When Darla Hit

Paul + Jean,
I hope you enjoy
my book and recognize
your daughter as Colleen.
Love, Rosalie
R. Grace Comyns

r. grace comyns

When Darla Hit

A Ridley-Brook Publication

Ridley-Brook Publishing
Waterbury, VT 05676

First Edition

When Darla Hit is a work of fiction.

Cover Design by Kitty Werner, RSBPress LLC

10 digit ISBN 0-9785281-0-7
13 digit ISBN 978-0-9785281-0-2

SAN 850-8860

Library of Congress Control Number: 2006937765

9 8 7 6 5 4 3 2 1

Acknowledgments

I would like to thank the following friends, mentors, and professionals for their help with this book: Erin Campos, Steve Carlson, Joseph Citro, Laurie McCarthy, Marie Merriam, Ann Monte, Amy Souza, and Kitty Werner.

And: Valerie Burd, Brittany Campos, Val Carmley, Janet LaPan, Doris Leitzell, Sandy Morningstar, Chici Pike, Ray and Susan Plagge, Doris Rondeau, Dona and Jerry VanAsdale, Kirsten Wiley, and Ron and Carolyn Ziara-Threlfall for their unfailing encouragement, inspiration, and support.

In loving memory of my parents, Marion and Nelson; my sister, Margaret; my brothers William, Lawrence, James, and Donald; and my dear friends, Claire Ellen Blodgett and Margaret Newton Simon.

When Darla Hit is a work of fiction. Although the historical events took place, and the second chapter is based in reality, any other similarities are just that. Whatever its faults, I take responsibility for every word and for my humble attempt to show what I understand to be life's most important lessons.

Chapter 1

1977 — Back Roads And Bogeymen

How could I let such a day go by? Autumn colors like this you can only dream about unless you're in New England, especially Vermont—pictures do this place no justice. We still travel over dirt roads here; real back roads, unpaved and often uncared-for, lined with pastures and rolling hills and trees filled with wondrous color supporting ancient stone walls, wild flowers peeking out from beneath the rocks. I decided to drive down one of those roads, have a smoke, and enjoy my last bit of time alone. The children were at my sister's house, and she wasn't expecting me for hours. Soon enough, I'd just be Mommy again.

I had spent the better part of the day at a ski lodge in Stowe, attending a dreaded construction seminar. Driving over the winding mountain roads made me want to keep driving, but I forced myself to pull into the parking lot and walk to the entrance. I wanted to leave from the moment I walked in; as always fighting the anxiety caused by crowded rooms, yet reminding myself that business owners need to network. What a waste of time, sitting cooped up inside a stuffy room filled with people whose main goal in life was to get rich. Still, I felt compelled to endure the event.

The seminar organizers fed us well and then bored us nearly to sleep. Speakers advised us how to succeed in the hostile world of general contracting by participating in the transportation agency's Disadvantaged Business Enterprise programs. Being one of the few women in the state who owned and operated a construction company, I had been asked to participate. Most of the state's DBE's were run by men who took full advantage of the fact that they had a drop of Native American, African, or Hispanic blood. A number of women were listed as 51 percent owners on paper, but most of those ladies had little to do with running the business. Feeling far more swamped than disadvantaged, I had no time for the politics and didn't agree with the premise. What we needed, in my opinion, was a system that kept the big guys honest, regardless of their gender or origin.

After shaking a few hands and thanking the committee chairman for my invitation, I explained that I had family commitments and wouldn't be staying for the cocktail reception. Delighted to be out of there, I couldn't stop smiling as I walked across the parking lot toward my new company truck, an F150 the color of a blue lagoon at midnight, full moon. As I drove away, the sunlight streamed through the overhanging branches and rippled like water on the hood. The air felt fresh and clean, unlike other places I had lived over the years, making me question why I ever left this beautiful place. But at seventeen the beauty wasn't apparent to me; it's hard to feel joy and see wonder when you feel dark inside. Today I felt light inside, light and happy. Moving back home after all those years had definitely been the right thing to do. I was doing a good job raising my children by myself, and actually making progress in a field that is usually considered men's work. Being my own boss and the head of my household felt like success to me.

When the dirt road I drove down started to look more like a logging trail, I began to appreciate the truck's qualities. Even though the four-wheel-drive feature involved outside activation, it was good to know it was there if needed. Trees loomed huge with brilliant leaves and breezy motion, stray branches brushing against my truck as I made my way down the narrowing road. Slowing nearly to a stop, I leaned over and rolled up the window on the passenger side to prevent more twigs from popping through the window. I brushed off the seat and cranked up the music, singing along to J. J. Cale's *After Midnight* and strumming on the steering wheel as the truck crawled along.

Within a mile the trail opened to a clearing, an offbeat camping area or something to that effect—a dead end. I saw a beat-up Volkswagen bus, a rusted orange color. A man sat slumped in the driver's seat with his arm hanging out the window while another man leaned against the outside, curls of smoke rising from their cigarettes. The men looked even scruffier than the mangy dog tied to the back bumper, just beneath a New York license plate. The skull tattoo on the driver's forearm sent a chill down my spine, large and badly drawn, definitely an amateur job.

It had rained during the night, making the ground soft, with several large puddles and some deep ruts to maneuver. I turned down the music and passed the men, giving a slight nod of acknowledgment and driving slowly to avoid getting stuck. Wishing I had activated the 4WD when I thought about it, I turned the truck around on a dry patch of land about fifty feet beyond the men, and backed up a few yards to make sure I had a straight exit from the clearing. I locked the truck doors and reached behind the seat, feeling around until my hand touched the leather holster, which I unsnapped and placed on my lap. Just in case. Then I started driving slowly toward the only way out, past the two perilous-looking rednecks that seemed to be robbing me of my free afternoon.

"Stay cool, girl," I said quietly to myself as I drove forward. Maybe these guys were harmless, no sense freaking out for nothing. Both men stood outside their van now, watching me.

When I got within a few yards of them, the taller one stepped up to my truck and reached for the door handle on my side. He said, "What's your hurry, little lady?" as he tried to open the door, holding onto the handle and walking along with the truck. Even his voice was ugly. Glancing in my side view mirror, I saw the other guy approaching the back of my truck. I pressed lightly on the gas pedal and the tall, threatening man walked faster, still holding on.

"Oh, God help me," I whispered.

Because of the truck's height, I sat face-to-face with my attacker. His face looked even dirtier than his T-shirt, patches of grime and grease covering both, causing me to shudder again at the sight of him. The other guy jumped onto the back of my pickup just as I stepped on the gas, hitting a bump in my path and causing the truck to swerve. The leather case slipped from my lap as the gun fired, sending a bullet right through my door. Suddenly the man lost hold of the door handle, grabbing his right leg as he fell to the ground. My unwanted passenger bounced off the tailgate and rolled on his side in the mud.

Quickly jumping up, he ran to his friend's rescue, his fist waving in the air, yelling at the top of his lungs. "We'll get you, you fuckin' bitch!" The dog began to bark.

By the time I reached the main road I couldn't hear the engine over the pounding of my heart, a noise that seemed far louder than the gunshot from my small pistol. Without thinking, I turned off the road in the wrong direction. Quickly realizing my mistake, I looked for the first side road that would circle around toward my sister Claire's house. A good move, I thought, as the mud on my tires would likely fall off, leaving less of a trail by the time I reached pavement again.

I drove carefully but as fast as I could in case they were following me, too stunned to laugh or cry, driving with my hands clenched tight around the steering wheel. My entire body trembled as I pulled up and parked the truck near my sister's driveway, just out of sight from the house.

As I sat there, I imagined telling my best friend Colleen about what had just happened. The two of us had shared many adventures together, fearless as we explored back roads or hiking trails. But shooting a bullet into a redneck's leg, well, that was more of an adventure than either of us would have wanted. Collie hated guns; today would have blown her mind. We had driven many back roads similar to that one. Usually there wasn't a soul around, and the souls we did meet were of the friendly, harmless type. I was glad I'd had my pistol, yet I was well aware that if those misfits reported me to the police, I would probably be the one arrested...for shooting a firearm. Even though I was defending myself. The bullet was only a .25 caliber and probably hadn't done too much damage after passing through the heavy truck door. *It probably just grazed the bastard,* I reasoned.

After my hands stopped shaking, I started up the long driveway to retrieve Dawn and PJ. I decided not to mention the incident, hoping that the two creeps were too preoccupied planning their ambush to notice my license plate number, or too dumb to memorize it. I wasn't in the mood to hear the lecture about how I'm not careful enough, take too many chances and so on...and that would be before the sheriff even arrived. Then I would have to explain the hole in my door, and the gun.

I sat for a bit, accepting my sister's offer of a quick cup of tea. My brother-in-law asked if I felt all right after my sister mentioned that I looked pale.

"The seminar really wore me out," I lied.

My eight-year-old son, PJ, lay sprawled on the living room rug, obviously spent from playing with his cousins. He smiled when he saw me but didn't speak or move. Eleven-year-old Dawn joined us for tea, happy to be included by her favorite aunt the way her grandmother always had. Darkness was setting in as we got up to leave. Our cozy little house was an hour or so away and in the opposite direction, thankfully, from that dirt road.

I felt relieved that no one noticed the hole in my door, and that my children had not been with me that day. We often took side roads while traveling, stopping in picturesque places to enjoy the scenery or wade in a brook. On one long road trip, the three of us spent eleven days driving across the United States and Canada in a bright yellow van, the color so much like French's mustard that we joked about putting a pump on the roof. A mattress on the floor of the van was where we slept each night, unable to afford a motel, and with barely enough money for gas; the Canadian royal gallons nearly double the price I'd planned on. We cooked soy dogs and veggie burgers on roadside grills, and ate fruit, cheese, and sandwiches from our cooler, a gift from the friends we made at my job as district secretary for the Southland Corporation in Bakersfield, California. I moved there seeking greener grass, finding mostly dirt once again.

We had a wonderful time weaving our way across both countries. The kids hadn't fought much and I felt completely at peace, having decided to move home to Vermont. My mother had recently been diagnosed with diabetes and heart disease; I knew it was time to go home. The three of us didn't really like California, anyway. I'd been talked into moving there by a well-meaning brother who lived in Bakersfield and actually loved it there. Being from New England, I couldn't understand why anyone would voluntarily live in such a big, dusty city. The delightful smells of orange groves and eucalyptus trees did not make up for the extreme desert heat, or for us feeling so out of place.

The memories of our cross-country trip faded as we reached our house to find no sign of police or the rusted orange van. I hustled the kids inside and checked all the doors and windows in the house while they brushed their teeth and chattered about their day. After tucking them in, I went out to the truck to get my pistol, feeling very lucky to have a garage where the bright blue truck with a hole in the driver's door would not be spotted.

Many thoughts went through my head as I cleaned and reloaded the pretty little Beretta pistol. My friend Joe gave me the piece while the kids and I were living in a questionable neighborhood in New Haven, Connecticut a few years earlier. Being a divorce attorney, Joe had seen too many women fall prey to burglars or violent ex-husbands. His wife, Diane, taught me how to shoot and care for the gun.

My children were instructed to do the following if they came across any firearm: Stop, Don't touch, Go away, and Tell an adult. I threw away any toy guns they were given, much to the dismay of their uncles. Pretending to shoot someone was not my idea of play. My son was born just nine days before a man walked on the moon, shortly after the race riots that ravaged the country, and during another nasty war in a far-off land. Life seemed to have taken on an air of danger.

I became responsible for my children's security after their father, Paul Sr., left us to be with his girlfriend. I found work as a waitress to support the three of us, unsure of how my husband could live with himself, but quite sure that his leaving was the best thing that happened to me since I married him, other than the birth of our children. I probably would have stayed in that senseless, abusive marriage much longer if flirty old Elsie hadn't come along and scooped Paul and his shiny gold Corvette right up. How she loved to drive that car, especially with the top down.

For the first time since I met Paul, I didn't have to answer to him. We started dating shortly after I moved to Connecticut from Vermont. He bought me a diamond engagement ring three months into the relationship and he convinced me to marry him within a year, thus avoiding a tour in Vietnam. Two kids and a raised ranch later, he decided that our simple family life wasn't quite enough for his narcissistic self. Taking up with another woman was quite the ego booster for him, at least for a while.

Paul had known Roy and Elsie since high school. The attractive couple had recently discovered the fun pastime of "partying." That meant drinking a lot of alcohol and then fooling around with other couples. It was the early seventies; wife swapping had just come into vogue. The swinging lifestyle made its way clear across the country, from the shores of California to the suburbs of Connecticut and beyond. Paul became infatuated right away.

Having made very few friends in my isolated world of childcare and making sure the spaghetti sauce tasted absolutely perfect every Thursday night, I was intrigued by Elsie's disregard for propriety. She pouted to get her way with our husbands, scoffing at housework and poking fun at my subservience. After her son was born, I babysat for her and lent her my clothes while she secretly dated my husband. This small-town girl didn't fit into the suburban party scene, so the players simply left me out of it. Elsie's alcoholic husband didn't seem to care what anyone else was doing once he had enough to drink. While Roy went off drinking, and I cooked, cleaned, and cared for the kids, his wife and my husband "partied" together.

When Paul's sister finally told me about the affair, I realized how naïve and blind I had been. It felt humiliating to know that my husband flaunted his affair behind my back, actually bringing his mistress to visit his family and friends. Even though I suspected that something might be going on, I felt crushed when my suspicions were confirmed.

The love-struck couple left the state in haste once I found out. An old friend of Paul's shamed him into giving me power of attorney before they left. I'm sure my husband thought that everything, including his Corvette, would be waiting for him just the way he left it, when and if he decided to return. He would never dream that I might pull myself up and get on with life. After all, he had spent over seven years convincing me that I had no purpose in life other than that of being his wife and the mother of his children. Always meek and passive, I rarely voiced an unsolicited opinion, wanting my children to grow up in peace and harmony instead of the chaos and pain that I remembered from my own childhood. Being a mother demands strength, however, and I had grown strong enough to do what I thought was best for my children and myself.

Paul and Elsie returned after only a few weeks. With them was Elsie's two-month-old son, their affair having started when she was already pregnant. The colicky baby took the wind right out of their romantic sail and my husband returned, penniless and over forty pounds lighter. Paul was a thin man to begin with and losing so much weight caused his six-foot frame to look shrunken and depleted, his hooded eyes even more weary. His lawyer advised him that if he got back into our house with his luggage I would have no recourse but to let him stay, and, furthermore, I would probably want him back anyway.

I did not want him back, of that I was certain. Seven years of the anxiety Paul created by being condescending and critical, left me with low self-esteem, a ton of anger, and no love for the man. As Paul stood in the doorway talking about his lawful rights and how I should grow up and accept an occasional indiscretion, the memories of how he and Elsie used me and lied to me, came flooding back. I set about gathering the necessary belongings and instructed my three-year-old son and six-year-old daughter to use the bathroom and get ready to go for a ride. The kids didn't seem overly happy to see their father, almost as if they didn't recognize him in his weary, crumpled state. I knew they were scared and confused, as startled by his return as I was. I fought to stay calm as my insides were threatening to heave.

Before he ran off with Elsie, Paul raved that the only person in our household who meant anything to him was his son, Paul E. Tarrington, Junior. He walked around like a peacock when our son was born, and insisted on naming him after himself. That pride thing wore off within a few months, just as it had after our daughter was born.

Knowing that my baby girl, who loved her Daddy with all her heart, heard his horrible comment about his son being the only one who meant anything to him, cut my heart to shreds. He couldn't possibly have meant it. Dawn was a beautiful, smart, and loving little girl. Everyone adored her and in spite of what he claimed, I knew her father did too. We didn't realize she was awake during our quarrel. I had asked him to stay home that night, to help decorate the basement for Dawn's birthday party, which was to take place the following afternoon.

After her father stormed out that night, my precious, confused little daughter came to me and said, "Mommy, why doesn't Daddy love me? Is it because I colored on the walls that time? I promise I won't do it again."

With tears in my eyes, I told her, "No...oh, Honey, no. Daddy was just mad at me for not wanting him to go out. He didn't mean any of that; he was just angry. He loves you very much, I promise. This has nothing, not *one* thing, to do with you."

Now he was back, telling her that he loved her and that Mommy wouldn't let him live here. I knew the children were too young to understand, but I wasn't about to take their father back and give them a false sense of security that surely wouldn't last. Being abandoned once was enough.

After loading our bags into my old Mercury, I told the kids to say goodbye to their father so we could leave. When Paul tried to stop me and get me to "see reason," as he put it, I just shook my head and pushed my way past him and his brand new set of luggage. I quietly told him that he was welcome to the house since it would be in foreclosure soon, and that I wasn't going to spend a night in the same house with him ever again. Little did I know, I would soon face him in a night of terror, a night that could have ended it all.

Here it is, nearly six years later, and as I sit on my bed cleaning my gun, the memories remain vivid. I let them replay in my head as I feel the weight of the pistol in my hand, knowing the gun would not have helped me that night.

Paul had broken into our apartment a few weeks after the kids and I relocated. Awakened by a noise, I got out of bed to check on the children. I kissed their sleeping heads and tucked their blankets around their little shoulders, all the while unaware that Paul was hiding in the kitchen. He stood silently in a corner holding a large knife that he took from the drawer. As I walked into the dark kitchen to get some water, he grabbed me from behind and held the knife to my throat.

Through clenched teeth he said, "Now, you're going to listen to me, Ro. Do you understand?"

My voice shook and my body tensed as I held back my scream and whispered, "Paul, what are you doing? The kids are asleep; please don't scare them. Don't hurt me, please. I promise we'll talk. We'll work this out. Please...please."

Somehow I talked him down as sweat was running past my temples, mixing with tears, my wrists hurting from trying to keep his hand with the knife away from my throat. Blood trickled from a small cut on the side of my neck as he finally lowered the knife and placed it on the counter. It seemed as though he scared himself nearly as much as he scared me, and he left as quietly as he had entered. I stood shaking in my kitchen as I watched him drive away.

After I bolted the door and locked the window he had pushed open, I called Joe. He and Diane came over and stayed with me until morning. Joe called the police and filed a complaint, described the attack and stated that I was "bleeding profusely;" lawyer-speak. Paul was soon arrested and placed behind bars.

The real terror started after his sister Lilly bailed him out of jail. He began threatening the kids and me, calling several times each day, and often approaching us when we emerged from a grocery store or returned home. It became obvious that he was stalking us, following us whenever we left our tiny apartment. I begged him to leave us alone. I told him that the children were growing afraid of him, and that I needed some time to sort things out. I was terrified, for my children and for myself, so I filed a restraining order against him. Paul ignored the restraining order, and his threats and pleas continued as he tried to wear me down.

"If I can't have you, no one will. People make mistakes sometimes; it isn't fair to make me suffer any longer." "You are my wife and those are my children; they belong with me. You'll never be able to support them by yourself." "Everyone deserves a second chance." And so on.

I didn't feel that my husband deserved a second chance, and I was surprised to learn that from all those years of silent rage a fiery strength had grown inside of me. It felt good to be on my own. I knew I'd never take him back.

When Lilly realized how dangerous her brother had become, she stopped helping him. She had always been good to us, buying clothes for the kids and me, and helping me deal with Paul's selfishness and mental cruelty. Since my family lived two states away, Lilly had become like a sister to me. Paul never took me to visit my family in Vermont during all our years together; he never even met my father. My mother, bless her heart, managed to travel to see me, over eight hours by bus, when both of my babies were born. I felt too powerless to go against my husband's wishes or even to question his reasons, having been taught by the church that it's a wife's duty to love, honor, and obey her husband, forsaking all others, including her family. Turns out it's also the best way to diminish a woman's confidence.

After being warned by the police that he would be arrested again unless he complied with the restraining order, Paul stayed out of sight. Yet he continued to call me, often saying he had a gun to his head and threatening to pull the trigger if I didn't come to his motel room or where ever he was holed up at the time. Elsie had returned to her husband temporarily while Paul, who was trying desperately to rid himself of the debilitating guilt, decided what to do. It shocked him that I sold his precious Corvette while he was gone. He had left me with no money; what was I supposed to do? Aside from that loss, it must have been unbearable to lose the affection of his wife and children, after having taken it all for granted for so long.

The last time Paul called with a gun to his head, I phoned Lilly for advice once again. His previous cries for help resulted in my pleading with his friends or relatives to find him and talk him out of the violent action he was threatening. I didn't want him to die, just to accept what he had done and learn to live with it. This time, Lilly persuaded me to put the kids in the car and drive to her house. Per her instructions I returned Paul's call from a phone booth on the way, shaking like a leaf as I waited for him to answer.

"Paul, I can't take this anymore. Go ahead and pull the trigger, if that's what you have to do."

I hung up before he could respond, returned to my car, and drove to Lilly's.

He didn't pull the trigger. Within a few months, after contesting the divorce and losing to me in court, he left the state again. Lilly testified on my behalf at the divorce hearing. Paul moved away without paying back the money he had borrowed from his sister or the settlement that he owed me. He took all of the good furniture and any decent belongings that we accumulated during our marriage. The kids and I made do with what he left behind.

Once Paul and Elsie were settled in Florida, I forced myself to call him and ask for the child support he owed; I didn't ask for the alimony he'd been ordered to pay. Having been a stay-at-home Mom for so long, not allowed to work outside the house or even to entertain the idea, I possessed few employment skills. Waiting tables barely covered the rent and left me little time to seek a better job. I managed by swapping childcare with a co-worker, and I accepted any leftover food I was offered at the restaurant.

Paul had bragged to a mutual friend that he had a new Corvette, and that he and Elsie loved their condo. He was lounging by the pool when I called. His response sounded flippant, as though he considered my request a joke. "Ro, if you can't support those kids, send them to us and we'll take care of them."

Stunned by his cruel proposal and surprised by how quickly he had shed his guilt, it took a minute or two before I could speak. "Paul, you are one sorry excuse for a father. You can bet I'll work three jobs before I'll give up my children. You just take care of Elsie and *her* son."

There were times when I did work three jobs. As for child support, the court petitioned the state of Florida to attach Paul's salary for $35 per week, much less than the decree but enough to make our lives easier. I never felt any hardship in cutting corners, and my kids never seemed like burdens. Dawn and PJ were my blessings, my reasons for living, and my best friends. They depended on me, which gave me the courage and strength needed to raise them on my own.

We had moved to California after leaving Connecticut, because my brother Stan convinced me that jobs were plentiful there. Within a few months, I decided to stop looking for greener pastures and head home to the green mountains of Vermont. My mother's health improved, and my children flourished after the move. I found a job as field clerk for a local construction company, and enrolled in evening courses at the community college to learn business management. Eventually I managed to get my contractor's license, after convincing a local insurance agency to issue the bond required to bid on state projects. I ran the business from my basement, sub-contracting any projects I managed to win. And, Disadvantaged Business Enterprise or not, you had to be the low bidder in order to be awarded a contract.

The pungent smell of cleaning oil brought me around to the realization that I was still holding my gun. Worn out by the day's events and all the heavy memories, I closed my cleaning kit and placed my pistol in the catch-locked drawer of my nightstand before getting into bed.

I woke to the sound of birds singing and rays of sunshine filtering through my bedroom curtains, a sharp contrast from dreams filled with nefarious men and ferocious junkyard dogs chasing me in the dark. I was being shot at, and then I found myself drowning in a stormy sea. Waking up felt like being rescued from bloodthirsty sharks and slime-dripping sea monsters. I sat on the edge of my bed and stretched my arms, shaking my head as if to shake off the dream. Sometimes reality is the best escape.

After looking in on my sleepy heads, I locked the gun drawer and headed downstairs to make coffee. It felt good to know that my troubled dreams were private and that my children's dreams were most likely pleasant ones. They would sleep late since we had returned home well after their normal bedtime. They loved visiting their cousins, always wearing themselves out in the fresh country air, playing ball, picking apples, or sometimes riding a pony.

Even at ages eight and eleven, they still resembled angelic infants when they were sleeping. Waking hours brought the normal sibling rivalry, with PJ teasing his sister to tears at times. Being the only male in the household, he often tested my patience with his tough-guy attitude. Growing up without a father wasn't easy for either of them, and playing the role of both parents was often exhausting. But I loved them dearly, confident that they felt secure and happy with me. At the end of every day, whether easy or hard, it was all worth it.

Once a week we held a family meeting, each of them given the opportunity to express complaints and ideas, without interruptions. I smiled thinking about how mature they had become over the years. Statements such as, "She called me a bonehead," or, "He doesn't even ask before he takes my things," were becoming less frequent. Now the two were more apt to team up and persuade me to let them stay up later or allow them to spend the night at their friends' houses. They clearly loved each other even though they didn't like to show it.

As I poured my second cup of coffee, I noticed the sound of a loud vehicle working its way up my hill. I rushed to the side window and looked toward the road, my heart beating faster. It seemed a long time before the noisy vehicle came into view, close enough for me to see the old one-ton truck that my neighbor uses for hauling firewood. Winter was rapidly approaching; there was a frost just last night.

The pounding in my chest subsided as I walked across the room and turned on the radio. During the week my favorite station offered an eclectic mix of rock, blues, and jazz. On Sunday mornings they played classical music, evoking a spiritual ambiance of calm and peace, almost like a private mass without the Latin. Even household chores were done with an air of pleasant satisfaction. This Sunday I decided to forego my usual routine of laundry and vacuuming, and simply enjoy the day. Housework could wait, and I would make the kids their favorite breakfast of pancakes and sausages when they woke up hungry later on.

As I sat drinking my coffee and watching my neighbor unload his truck, a news brief was announced on the radio. Two men had been apprehended in a nearby county, after breaking into an empty home during the night. A neighbor noticed some lights on and an old Volkswagen bus parked in the driveway. Knowing that his neighbors were on vacation, he notified the police. The men were arrested and would be arraigned the next morning. Their arrest followed a string of burglaries in the area. Both men had recently been released from a New York State correctional facility, and one of them suffered a fresh gunshot wound to his leg.

I sighed with relief at the thought of the two men sitting in jail, and then thought about the hole in my truck door. I decided to use a magnetic sign to cover the hole instead of getting the door repaired. Less questions that way.

Outside my living room windows, the trees and bushes are heavy with dew. Tiny sparkles dance on the multi-colored leaves as sunshine fills the day with warmth and hope. Autumn has always been my favorite time of year. By next weekend the foliage will be at its peak and I'll take my dear mother on our annual fall ride, a custom we started shortly after I moved back home. It's always fun to take my mother places, because she so enjoys the going.

"Where would you like to go this year, Mom?" I had asked her the previous weekend.

She answered as she always did, "Oh, I don't care, Rosie. Any place you feel like driving will be just fine with me."

I smiled at the thought of her climbing up into the front seat of my pickup, knowing that she got such a kick out of riding in it. When I told her that I was planning to buy a truck for my business, she had turned her lips into a smiling frown and said, "I always liked Fords. Blue ones."

Shortly after that, I ordered a blue F150 pickup, brand new, the first new vehicle I'd ever owned.

This year I decided I would bring Mom to visit one of her sisters, my Aunt Viola, who lives way down a back road over past Maple Corner. We will keep our doors locked...and I'll make sure that my Beretta is carefully hidden behind the seat.

Chapter 2

Marion Matilda

That was one of the last foliage rides I would get to enjoy with my mother. She died a few years later, after a series of strokes. I still miss her, of course. She was the source of more wisdom and love than any other person I have ever known. Mom always told us we were from good peasant stock, proving it by bearing and raising thirteen children, and housing even more. My father often called her his Blackfoot squaw. Whether my mother actually had any Native American blood I've never known for sure, although her high cheekbones were evidence that she might. Family history shows my paternal great-grandmother to be of Iroquois descent.

My mother's parents were Scottish and French from what I knew. In our family, however, you didn't get to know much even if you asked. I usually didn't ask, or didn't listen; maybe I just wasn't interested then. Around our dinner table, the conversation seldom included us kids. The subjects of discussion were: people (sick, dead, or in trouble), chores, money, hunting, fishing, and politics. Arguments were not uncommon.

As a child I seldom had the opportunity to be alone with my mother. Once in a while, when I was sick, she would bring me tea or broth, especially if my older sister Mary was still at school. When Mary was home, she was the designated caregiver. Four children younger than me needed care, some not yet of school age, so there was always someone who needed something. Somehow, though, none of us were neglected too much or for too long.

Homemade remedies were administered when anyone got sick, my mother always knowing exactly what to do. Tea bags were placed over swollen eyes, crusted and closed from one malady or another. Blackberry roots were boiled to treat stomach ailments, mustard packs and herb poultices expertly prepared by her hands for back injuries or bouts of ringworm. It always amazed me that she knew so much, worked so hard, and yet never seemed to think of her lot in life as a hardship. Being the second oldest of fifteen children, she had been taught very well.

An amazing and slightly mysterious woman, there is still controversy over my mother's middle name, Matilda. Her birth certificate showed the letter I, with the rest of the name blacked out. Her social security card also appeared to have been altered. Aunt Jessie, my mother's youngest sister, told me she thought Mom's middle name was Mildred. No one seems to know if or why my mother changed her middle name to Matilda, or whether it really was Matilda and someone used Mildred by mistake.

Another mystery is her birth date. As far as we knew, she was born on March 15, 1910, but the record that shows her middle name as Mildred, shows her birth date as March 18, 1909. She may have needed to be eighteen to get married, probably without her parents' permission. In the scheme of things, when she was born and whether her middle name was Matilda, Mildred, or Irene, doesn't really matter. Her children would have loved her as dearly by any name. She was our caring, intelligent, and humble mother.

And...she fed us. A large garden provided food to eat, and enough for canning and filling the root cellar. Mom always dumped her wash water, drained from the ringer washing machine and laced with shavings of homemade lye soap, into the garden, growing beets and turnips the size of cabbages and cabbages as big as basketballs. Not exactly organic gardening, although it might have been.

My father and older brothers hunted and fished often, bringing home a large variety of wildlife to be cleaned and cooked. Mom could make anything taste good or at least edible, even fried salt pork and the scorch gravy she made by browning some flour in a greased iron skillet and adding water, salt and pepper. From bear meat to tripe, there seemed to be foolproof recipes in her head for cooking food the best possible way, making do with what she had.

She baked breads and beans, and canned jar after jar of corn, tomatoes, and green beans from our garden. Delicious sweet pickles made from huge cucumbers, with tiny sacks of spices tucked inside the jars, were lined up on the cellar shelves. On holidays and occasional weekends, usually when company was expected, my mother made pies from whatever became available. Every pie she baked, whether mincemeat, apple, or pumpkin, looked, smelled, and tasted incredible.

I don't remember ever going to bed hungry but we certainly were not overfed, nor were we offered snacks between meals. Sometimes late at night, after everyone had gone to bed and our father's bedroom door was closed, my younger sister Meg and I would sneak downstairs to get saltine crackers or a slice of bread, which we coated with sugar and then sprinkled with water so that the sugar wouldn't fall off. We would tiptoe past the Home Comfort stove and into the pantry, a small back room that housed the refrigerator and the Hoosier cabinet that held dry goods, spices, and bread. Mom's bedroom was on the other side of the house; she rarely heard anything until her four-thirty wake-up hour.

Food could not be wasted, so we weren't allowed to cook while we were growing up. My sisters and I helped in the kitchen by peeling potatoes, doing the dishes, and sweeping the well-worn linoleum floor. My brothers shoveled snow or mowed the grass, chopped wood, and filled the wood boxes. We all helped in the garden and most chores were done willingly, except for plucking chickens. That job took all the fun out of watching the goofy birds run around without heads.

Feeding everyone, twelve to fifteen people at most meals, must have been a real chore, but my mother seemed to take it all with a grain of salt. No one complained about what was placed on our large farm table, as we sat on unmatched chairs in an amazingly orderly fashion. With our father at the head of the table, we didn't need to be reminded to behave or to use proper manners. When guests came, we kids were fed after the adults had eaten. Usually, though, the table provided enough room for the immediate family, plus a few extras. There always seemed to be enough to go around.

I'm told that during harder times, before I can remember, food was not as plentiful and life was much tougher. My older brothers were not allowed to attend school after eighth grade, at which time they were put to work to help support the family. A family that continued to grow every two years or so, until our mother's childbearing years were over.

During my early childhood, our family lived on a 900-acre homestead in North Calais. The large barn didn't contain cows, but we had a few horses, some chickens, and a couple of goats. There always seemed to be a chainsaw humming, and logs being hauled away. I don't remember knowing why we had to move; I was only six then. From what an older brother told me later on, losing the property had something to do with keeping one of my father's brothers out of jail. We moved to Woodbury, and then to Cabot after our house in Woodbury burned down. Our father went to work at a car dealership in Barre, selling Studebakers and Mercedes Benz. Nearly every night a new car was parked in front of our old house, which was covered with yellowish brown tarpaper shingles and attached to a shed that was nearly as large and even more rickety-looking. It seemed pretty strange to have a shiny new car in front of our house, giving the place sort of a country ghetto appearance.

Our town was very small, no actual ghetto or other side of the tracks, train tracks that is. The lower village was home to a lumber mill, a small general store, and a handful of older homes and farms. The more prominent upper village was where the school, town hall, and post office were located. We lived in the lower village. The Winooski River ran past both villages. "Winooski" is an Abenaki Indian word meaning "where wild onions grow." The plants grow along the river's banks as it rambles westward toward Lake Champlain.

The riverbank, located in a field across the road from our house, was one of my favorite places to spend time. I sat there often, watching the water as it washed happily over rocks and branches, going somewhere and going nowhere at the same time. When I wasn't watching the water or reading a book, I often climbed trees or hiked through the nearby pastures or woods. I called my pastime "exploring," and spent hours on end lost in my own little world in the woods. Sections of the forest became rooms, pine needles serving as carpets, and overhanging branches as ceilings. I pretended that the birds and squirrels were my friends, like Freckles in the Gene Stratton-Porter book of the same name. I picked flowers and tucked the small bouquets into tree stumps to decorate my rooms, and I ate the wild berries and nuts that I had seen my mother and my older siblings harvest.

I didn't like spending time in our crowded home, and I was seldom missed when I was gone. With the exception of an occasional argument with Meg or my brother Dean, the two closest to my age, I tried to stay out of sight and out of trouble. The leather strap that hung by my father's bedroom door was a strong reminder for all of us not to step out of line. Called a razor strap, it was used to sharpen the straight razor he shaved with, and to discipline his children. Its abrupt sting produced red welts on our legs and a sense of terror in our hearts.

His bedroom was also his office and the place where he repaired clocks and watches at night, a trade passed down from my grandfather Silas. The only telephone was in his room, so whenever I had a call from a school friend, I was forced to go in there. My father would sometimes detain me, unless I managed to hang up fast and run out of the room while his back was turned. The thought of his touches made me tremble in fear, as did the thought of him closing that door while I was captive. The memory of smelling Ben-Gay, cigar smoke, and whisky, sometimes returns when I hear a telephone ring or force myself to make a call. It has gotten somewhat easier over the years, but the anxiety never really goes away. I can't think about my father without remembering the smells in his room, and the feelings of shame, despair, and isolation. Anything good about him was clouded over by the bad. The good was that he did provide shelter, for his family and for others.

My father's mother came to live with us for a time when I was very young. I didn't know why and I don't remember asking. Many years later I learned that our grandfather had gone to prison after being in a barroom fight. Someone was killed, and he had shouldered the blame so that another man with small children could stay with his family. Whether that was all true, I don't really know. When I think of Grandpa, I see him sitting at his workbench fixing clocks, or in his yard weaving baskets out of strips of wood that were pounded from an ash tree. I always wanted my own basket, but he never offered me one and I wouldn't have dared to ask. He made them to sell, not as gifts. He was taller than my father, but with the same white hair and gruff exterior.

Grandmother appeared frail yet wielded a sharp tongue. She always seemed to be in a bad mood when she lived with us, which may have had something to do with her husband being incarcerated. She never once got my name right whenever she spoke to me or asked me to bring her something, which wasn't often. I always wondered why she didn't just call me Rosie like the rest of my family did. Instead she turned my given name, Rosalie, into Rosalyn, Roseanne or Rosemary, or some other variation of the name. She never laughed or joked about it, just couldn't seem to get it right. Her name was Elizabeth; most people called her Lizzy.

My mother's father died when I was quite young. I remember him as a small, bald headed man with a ring of red hair around the baldness, and a walnut-sized bump on the top of his head. He fathered fifteen children with my grandmother, and rumor had it that he left them for rather long periods of time to fend for themselves. During those times, Grandma made and sold dandelion wine and raised vegetables and chickens to feed her family. She managed to protect her home with a double-barreled shotgun and a .22 caliber rifle for scaring off critters. When her husband came home in a horse-drawn wagon after being gone for a year or so, she calmly told him to feed the chickens while she started supper. Anyway, that's the story I heard.

My maternal grandmother was Irish or Scottish, Rouse and Stewart her family names. Stout and serious, with deep-set eyes, you could tell she was a strong and trustworthy woman. Very superstitious, she believed that killing a spider in her house, or breaking a mirror—God forbid, would surely bring on years of strife. How that would have been different from the life she knew, I do not know. My strongest memory of Grandma Clara, (her middle name was Belle and her husband's name was Clarence), is of watching her hanging out the laundry near the most brilliant deep purple lilac bush I have ever seen. It bloomed every spring next to her antiquated home, the smell as sumptuous and intoxicating as an expensive French perfume. I have never seen another one quite that color or come across a fragrance that compares.

The walls of my childhood home held pictures of the Kennedy brothers, John and Robert, lined up on the living room wall, right next to some artist's depiction of Jesus. A large portrait of Franklin D. Roosevelt hung over my father's roll-top desk. My father didn't vote, simply instructing his wife how to vote as if she were his proxy with no vote of her own. All she had to do was pull the Democrat lever after all; it didn't matter who was running for office. When he learned she voted Republican against his orders (he overheard my brother-in-law joking about it), he was forced to accept the fact that his wife was her own woman.

That acceptance did not come easily or quietly, but my mother always held her own. My father would often rave on and on for some reason or other, raising his voice and swearing, but I never saw him hit her. She would shake her head and shrug her shoulders, as if almost amused at his tirade. Eventually she'd say, "Oh, Nelson...shut up." And sometimes, he did. She not only looked like her mother, she learned how to deal with her husband just as her mother had.

I lived in fear of my father's wrath, keeping out of his way as much as I could. During the times he wasn't at home, I grew braver and more visible, sometimes even acting like I was in charge.

One day my brother Edwin was drunk, which wasn't unusual, especially on the weekend. If the old man kept the boys busy during the week, they usually didn't start drinking until night. By then, us younger kids would be safe in bed if we were smart. The toilet was outside the kitchen in the attached shed, so you made sure you went to the bathroom before going to bed and didn't drink too much water or cool-aide. Otherwise, you might have to walk through that kitchen, past a table full of male relatives and their friends who were drinking beer, playing cards, telling stories, or fighting. The fighting always scared us, so most of us learned not to be seen *or* heard.

On that hot, dusty, summer day; a Saturday I think, because liquor wasn't sold on Sundays back then, Ed decided he was going to take Dad's old pickup, probably to buy more beer. My mother was nearly always home, but on that day my father took her into town or on a rare visit to see a relative. For some reason, at the age of eleven or maybe twelve, I decided I should stop my brother from taking the truck. I knew he'd been drinking when he took the keys from the cupboard, dropping them twice on his way out the door. And I could smell alcohol.

"Edwin!" I yelled as I ran after him. "Dad doesn't want anyone to use that truck, I heard him say so before he left."

I scooted past him and stood blocking the driver's door, my arms folded across my chest. At first my brother, who was nearly twice my age, just ordered me out of his way. When I refused to move he started pushing me, not hard enough to knock me down but hard enough to hurt. As we were yanking shirts and hitting at each other, my father's car pulled into the yard. I was relieved, yet almost afraid that I would be the one in trouble. Ed slammed me a good one and staggered off. My father didn't say a word, just took the keys and walked inside the house.

My mother told me later that I shouldn't be fighting with anyone bigger than me, because I could get hurt. She also said, "I'm proud of you for standing up to your brother. He shouldn't be driving when he's drinking."

That was the first time in my life that I ever remember being praised by anyone in my family. Having such a large family, my mother was always busy. She cooked, cleaned, and put up with relatives and non-relatives living with us in our ramshackle old house. Being praised or even being called by the correct name seemed very special to me at the time.

Maybe on that Saturday, although I suspect it happened much earlier, I took on what my therapist calls "diplomatic positioning" in my family. I left home at age thirteen to attend high school in another town. My father was very angry when he noticed, after a week or so, that I was gone. He yelled at my mother for letting me go, furious at my older brother for taking me. St. Monica's was a Catholic school and I thought I wanted to become a nun, which, according to the parish priest, would ensure a ticket to heaven for both of my parents. By the time I finished school I had become disillusioned with the church, and my mystic dreams of sisterhood evaporating with my faith.

In my sophomore year, I answered an ad for a babysitting job and left my brother's home to work for a wonderful woman named Doris. She had seven children, ranging in age from eight months to twelve years. Her husband was an alcoholic. The church denied her the right to divorce her abusive husband or to use birth control. She worked the night shift at a local factory to feed her children and pay the rent, while most of her husband's wages were used to support his favorite bar and grille. I came straight from school each day to care for the children so Doris could get a few hours of sleep before she left for work. At the age of thirty-seven, she suffered a heart attack. I missed a few weeks of school, and actually would have quit school to help her if she had let me. Her husband seemed annoyed that she missed so much work.

The family moved away in my senior year, and Doris eventually left both the church and her husband. I never understood the laws of the church; why the rules changed over the years to allow the wealthy to get annulments, or make it okay to eat meat on Fridays, and no longer essential to cover our heads in church. I figured that if man could change the laws of God, then man must have made them. It was all very confusing to me; I loved the church and wanted to believe in it.

During the time I lived with Doris, my father would sometimes send an older brother to bring me home for the weekend, especially if he needed his taxes filed or an insurance form filled out. That may have been his way of making me pay for my freedom, or getting back at me for escaping his abuse. I was quite certain it wasn't because he missed me, although he may have. He had always called me Rosa, and then took to calling me Gypsy Rosa Lee, or just Gypsy because I was so often away from home, accepting any offer to stay someplace else. I found jobs from the time I was ten—babysitting, picking strawberries, cleaning houses, or peeling pulp. It didn't matter what or where, as long as it was somewhere else.

Standing up for myself, speaking my mind, was not something that my father appreciated. So I learned to keep my mouth shut and stay away from him. I've always felt bad about leaving my four younger siblings back then, but I was a child myself, trying to survive. Thanks to my brother Earl, I was given the chance to leave home; maybe make something of myself. It didn't take long to decide whether to go once I was given the opportunity, even with a few strings attached. The free babysitting and four years of religious brainwashing didn't harm me all that much, and I have always appreciated my brother's good intentions. In many ways I regretted not staying home to help my mother cope, and to help my little sisters and brothers grow up. At the time I wasn't aware that I could make a difference, but over the years I've felt haunted by that realization. Earl always felt bad that he hadn't been able to take Meg away too.

I never returned to live with my family, leaving to take a job in Hartford, Connecticut three days after I graduated in 1964. I hadn't wanted to stay in Vermont and marry some immature idiot like most of my friends were doing, so I moved to Connecticut and married one there.

Edwin, even though he drank to excess, was really a good brother to me most of the time, as were all the others. He never mentioned our fight and we always got along fine after that, even when he was drinking. I may have earned his respect that day.

He had already earned my respect, during sober times when he worked hard and helped care for our family. Ed had the least education of all, in bed for two years with rheumatic fever as a child, he never even finishing grade school. His was a difficult life that ended at age sixty-three, when his tractor tipped over on him while he was dragging logs through the woods near his home.

All of my brothers and sisters grew up to be kind, hard working adults. It's unfortunate that I didn't get to know them very well until I was an adult too.

My sister Meg was less than two years younger than me. She was born prematurely at home, weighing only a few pounds. Mom kept my infant sister alive by focusing all of her love and attention on her weak little baby, sitting by the wood stove for days and days while nursing her tiny daughter to health. Meg was sickly while she was growing up, finally diagnosed with COPD, Chronic Obstructive Pulmonary Disease, when she was forty-six. Her lungs had not developed properly, and smoking cigarettes only made matters worse. After her condition was diagnosed, I realized that our mother might have been nursing me while she was pregnant with my sister. Feeling overwhelmingly guilty, it took months of therapy to convince me that my guilt was unfounded. Meg was the last baby to be born at home. Our mother, by then in her forties, gave birth to her last three babies in the closest hospital.

Before Meg died, shortly after her fifty-second birthday, she confided that she felt guilty knowing that our mother never had time for me after she was born. That thought had never occurred to me, but it may have been the reason I learned to be so independent from such an early age. Secretly, I thought it might also have been the reason that my mother never noticed how my father treated me, and my sister Mary. Abuse changes who you are as a person; it alienates you from others. Mary and I have never spoken about the pain our father caused us, and we probably never will. Five years older than me, she left home shortly before I did and I seldom hear from her. She was such a good sister when I was growing up, always helping care for us younger kids. She was the first girl in the family, the seventh child, preventing the birth of a seventh son. I think her childhood was probably much harder than mine. It usually is hardest for the oldest girl in a large family, so much expected of her and with a mother too busy to protect her. Life was no picnic for the older boys, either. My father's favorite expression was, "There's nothing wrong with you that a good days work won't fix."

My mother gave birth every couple of years for twenty-six years, and that was the only life she knew. Somehow she managed to have a smile on her face most of the time. It didn't seem to be a false smile, although my sister-in-law Janet once told me she suspected that my mother suffered from bouts of depression; something else I didn't know as a child, although I do remember days when she didn't come out of her bedroom. We were always told that she had a headache and not to make any noise.

One of the few times I ever saw my mother cry was after our house in Woodbury burned down. In addition to all of our clothing, personal items, and every stick of furniture, she lost all of her treasured family photographs. Aunt Edith, her sister-in-law and best friend, brought her earrings to try and cheer her up. After the fire, in which thankfully no one was seriously hurt, my family lived in an abandoned schoolhouse for several months. Some of us kids went to stay with whatever relative or neighbor offered to take us. I was taken by our school bus driver, and might have stayed with his family for good if I had been allowed to. They seemed so normal and so nice, and only *four* people lived there. His wife and daughters treated me well, and life seemed much easier in their home. When my father found another house to move into, I was returned to my family. It's doubtful that my mother had anything to say about where we moved, but it would be her home for the rest of her life.

After my father died, my mother embraced her freedom, becoming far more independent than she had ever dreamed of being. She never learned to drive because on her first attempt to do so, she backed into a utility pole. My father never let her try again. She had been dependent on him to take her places, which he seldom did. He paid the bills and bought the necessary supplies, keeping a tight hold on his wallet, which probably never held much money.

Once on her own, my mother enjoyed going shopping, to auctions and church bazaars, or on a ride to almost anywhere. My older brothers always made sure that my mother had enough money, as did my other siblings and I, once we had some of our own. She always had plenty of offers for rides, either from one of her many children, or from Uncle Frank and Aunt Edith. I can't remember her ever turning down an invitation to dinner, or an opportunity to visit almost anyone. During the last fifteen years of her life, she suffered from diabetes and heart disease. Meg lived nearby and visited twice a day to give my mother her insulin shots and make sure she ate right. Mom lost nearly all of her vision in both eyes, which was one of the few complaints we ever heard from her. She could no longer read a book, cook a meal, or even make herself a cup of tea. The bright colored leaves of her favorite season were now dull and barely visible.

Since childhood, Mom had helped care for others, and now she must be cared for. That wasn't something she enjoyed, but she kept her positive spirit and good nature most of the time. She once told my brother Earl, "There's no need to worry about things; life always turns out the way it's supposed to." Such a lesson in faith, and one she lived by. She had a delightful sense of humor, often goofing on herself or making a joke of someone's foul attitude, or some complaint she found ridiculous.

Meg passed away just over ten years after our mother's death. She was always closer to our mother than I was, than anyone was, I think. They must have formed a very strong bond while she was growing up. It would have broken my mother's heart to see how badly her fragile little daughter suffered during the last five years of her life.

My sister and I didn't get along well as children. I was never sure if Meg was jealous of me for being older and healthier, or if she was just angry and confused, maybe even for the same reasons that I felt angry and confused. I've always wondered if I could have kept her from smoking cigarettes when she was a teenager, or whether she would have smoked more just to spite me. None of that matters now. We grew closer as we got older, even closer during her dying years, and I was at her side as much as I could be.

Our youngest sister, Claire, was one of Meg's constant caregivers, her own health going downhill from the stress of watching one of her big sisters succumb to such a dreadful disease, and from all the hours of work that were added on to her already heavy workload. I have grown to admire my baby sister very much, and I regret not being there when she was growing up. She reminds me of our mother.

I am the only daughter in our family to be divorced, although my mother was divorced after a very brief marriage, before she married my father. I always wondered why she married my father; he was probably a nice young man at the time. I knew the reasons she stayed with him, all thirteen. My mother once explained that she had so many babies because of ignorance, a self-criticism that wasn't at all valid. No birth control pills were available to her; however, my father could have used condoms. Perhaps they seemed too expensive for him to buy. That, or he just didn't believe that there could be another baby, and another. I was the ninth of their thirteen children, born on the eleventh day of the eleventh month, at 11:11 p.m. Veterans Day, 1946.

My mother did the best job she could, raising her many children as well as several grandchildren. She stayed strong and helped others who were weak. Her second son died from pneumonia around age two, and her sixth son at age thirty-three after suffering from kidney disease for several years. She was not around to see her third daughter and two more sons die, her first born living to the age of seventy. Her youngest son became an alcoholic in his teens, now weak and ill with diabetes, Crohn's disease, and a number of other serious ailments. Geary never left home.

Dad used alcohol to keep his sons under his thumb, or maybe to reward them for working so hard. He also used alcohol to sooth his pains, to drown his sorrows, and to forget about his shortcomings and failures, most likely. It's obvious to me now that the money spent on tobacco and spirits contributed to our poverty, not the only reason by any means. It couldn't have been easy supporting so many. Our father taught us all to work hard and to keep our problems to ourselves, pride being another sin that didn't seem to register with the old man.

Our mother taught us by example to be strong and to have faith, not because she was a religious woman but because she was a righteous one. We may not have been encouraged to be honest about our feelings, but we certainly learned better than to steal or tell lies. Most likely Mom had her own secrets and sorrows, which she kept to herself as she had been taught.

The gentle goodness and strength of character that our mother passed on will stay with us always, her genes being the purest form of inheritance. If there is a heaven, Mom is certainly there, along with my beautiful little sister and four of my nine brothers. I wouldn't put money on whether Dad's up there, and it isn't my place to judge. Most abusers have been abused; all any-one can do is try to break the cycle, and he very likely did try.

Life is a journey, an opportunity to learn and to understand, to have faith, and to forgive. No one knows where the journey will lead or when it will end. My mother's journey lasted for eighty years, leaving her children a legacy of love, strength, and honor.

Chapter 3

Three Strikes And Lotsa Balls

Loneliness is not being alone, for then ministering spirits come to soothe and bless. Loneliness is to endure the presence of one who does not understand.

— *Elbert Hubbard*

It's amazing what a person will put up with just to sleep next to a warm body, sometimes even a cold one. Some of our most solitary moments are spent next to another person. The Bible teaches us that marriage forms a sacred union, making two people as one. But without real intimacy, which can only develop from deep love and friendship, a marriage can be an empty shell that harbors pain and loneliness, offering little happiness or contentment.

After Paul was out of my life, with the exception of occasional phone calls to arrange trips and visits for the kids, I realized that I was far less lonely without a husband. Yet it bothered me that my children didn't have a decent father figure. After a few years passed, long enough to forget some of the lessons I had learned, I married a man named Charles. We met through mutual friends, several years before we dated. Nothing that I can remember could have warned me what a terrible mistake it would be to marry him. He appeared to be a virtuous person, one with my best interests in mind.

Charles attended a Baptist church, and he insisted that God told him to marry me. Of course I wondered why God hadn't said anything to *me* about that, but I reasoned that I wasn't as close to Him since I no longer had any religious affiliation. Charles refuted my suggestion that we try living together first, saying that he didn't want to live in sin. He promised to be a faithful husband, help raise my children, and make my life easier.

When I asked my mother for advice, confessing to her that I wasn't sure I loved him, she looked at me as if to say, "Love is something that happens in books." What she actually said was, "You need a husband and your children need a father. Charlie seems like a good enough man."

I couldn't argue with that. We were married in a lovely little chapel, attended mostly by his family and a few close friends. My mother wasn't feeling well, my father didn't attend weddings, and my brothers lived too far away. Two weeks before Christmas, it was a busy time for my younger sisters, who made and sold wreaths and craft items to help support their families. A beautifully decorated wreath made from balsam and princess pine hung on my front door, and lovely crocheted snowflakes adorned my Christmas tree. Gifts instead of presence.

Joe and Diane drove up from New Haven, proud that I had asked Joe to walk me down the aisle; actually Diane's idea, one I thought was brilliant. My friends had never met Charles, but they arrived with open minds and sincere wishes that my second marriage would be far happier than my first.

As the organ music began to play and we prepared to walk down the aisle, Joe turned to me and said, "This doesn't feel right, Rosalie. Are you sure you want to marry this guy? And in a church, yet."

I laughed softly and gave him a hug, happy that he was there and concerned about me. I told him not to worry, that everything would be fine.

Joe's concerns turned out to be legitimate. The very next day, my new husband became a domineering tyrant, as if someone flipped a switch. Several of my friends later told me that they feared they would never see me again once I married Charles. I wondered how I could have been blind to what others saw so clearly. From the day we were wed, Charles set the rules and expected them to be followed. I was instructed not to leave the house until the beds were made and the dishes were done, things I normally did anyway.

At first I tried to joke with him and get him to lighten up, but that only caused him to become more tyrannical and threatening. If I came home a few minutes late from work or shopping, I'd find him in a pacing frenzy, questioning where I had been and what I had been doing. His deep blue eyes penetrated like lasers, piercing and dangerous.

He was equally as rigid with Dawn and PJ, insisting that his stepchildren sit and listen to him read the Bible every Wednesday night, PJ usually falling asleep within minutes, reprimanded for his lack of interest. We were bullied into going to church every Sunday morning, visiting his family or mine on alternate Sunday afternoons. The only exception was when he chose to go hunting or ice fishing. The kids and I relished those times, having decided during our first private family meeting after the wedding, that we should leave him as soon as their school year ended. We would need to find a safe place to hide; until then we would deal with it, together. He had fooled us all.

Charlie was a real man's man, macho to the core; our freezer held fish, venison, and bear meat. Just over three months after our marriage, he drove his jeep too far out on a frozen lake one foggy Sunday afternoon. The ice wasn't as thick as he calculated, even though he fished from the same spot just two weeks earlier. I felt relief and little else when I was informed of his untimely death. Husband number two could no longer hold my children and myself as hostages. I was left with the realization that I had married two men that I didn't even love, just because it seemed like the right thing to do at the time. Being a widow felt strange, unearned, as most blessings are.

Over the next few years, men came and went, mostly as friends, now and then as lovers. I was cautious not to let anyone get too close. Most of my time was spent working and caring for my children. My business had suffered during my brief marriage to Charles, but was now getting back on track. I had recently negotiated a lucrative bridge contract with the State of Vermont and the Town of Warren. When my friend Bette suggested that we celebrate my success, I agreed to meet her at a local club.

The band was excellent and we were having a great time, my first outing in months. Glen spotted us from across the room, then came over and bought us a drink. Bette had dated him in high school and she appeared almost giddy to see him again. Even though she was now married, she acted annoyed when he turned his attention to me. He asked me to dance and I accepted, ignoring Bette's warning glances, which I took for jealousy.

Not only was Glen a good dancer, he was bold and amusing. While we were on the dance floor, he actually stole a kiss from me. I pulled away laughing, surprised at his cheekiness. "Whoa, Buddy. You don't even know me."

"Yeah, I do," he said, a big grin on his face. "You just don't remember me. You went to St. Monica's, right? We met a few times, at basketball games. I used to hang around with Big Bobby Bonello, and you were friends with his sister. You wouldn't give me the time of day when I tried to talk to you. I couldn't figure out whether you were stuck-up or just bashful. So, which is it?"

I did remember Big Bobby, the tallest guy on our high school basketball team. Basketball games were the only social events allowed at our school that didn't directly involve the church. I had no recollection of meeting Glen. At the time I still planned to enter the convent; he attended a public high school—not even a good Catholic boy.

Glen told me that he recently returned from an engineering contract in Kuwait, to find that his wife was having an affair. He left without the usual fuss, after agreeing to child support and weekly visitations. Since his family had lived without him for over six months, seeing him on a weekly basis worked fine for everyone, including him. He was having fun, playing the field and getting back into the music scene. When he asked if I'd go out with him sometime, I told him I wasn't interested in dating a man who had an ex-wife and three kids.

After that night, Glen became obsessed with the idea of winning me over. Bette refused to give him my number, but he eventually tracked me down at my office, which was no longer in my basement. I ended up spending the next five years with Glen. Five years of him drinking and gambling, five years of other women falling all over him. Even though he wasn't a particularly handsome man, his mischievous charm won him lots of attention, including mine. He was a good man when he was sober, and I fell in love with him during the sober times. He was affectionate, helpful, and fun to be with.

We were married in our living room after we lived together for almost two years. All five children were present, and some nice old guy, a local Justice of the Peace, managed to make it up our hill in a snowstorm to do the honors. I can't even begin to explain why I agreed to marry Glen. Maybe it felt like he was rewarding me for putting up with his ill-behaved children every weekend, not to mention his greedy, manipulative ex-wife. He certainly wanted to make sure I would continue to put up with him; I was the best little enabler he could ever find. We didn't go on a honeymoon or even leave town, but he did take me to a different bar that night.

From the time we began living together, my modest home accommodated Glen and his kids, more than doubling the household's former population on weekends. His daughters slept in Dawn's room, and his son shared quarters with PJ. Even though my kids and I did our best to tolerate the behavior of three very spoiled younger children, it wasn't fair to expect all that sharing. It became more and more difficult as my teenagers grew older and needed their space. None of us were able to hide our disappointment, our family meetings abandoned as we loosened the bonds we shared for so long. The intrusion of another family destroyed our privacy and peace of mind. The love we felt for Glen did not make up for our losses.

During those years, I struggled to find inner strength and to be healthier, totally convinced that my unhappiness was self-induced. I fought to stop the depression that seemed to be overtaking my life, trying everything from yoga and chiropractics, to herbal remedies and aromatherapy. On the day the Challenger spacecraft blew up, the end of January 1986, I was in a doctor's waiting room with what felt like a refrigerator on my chest. The horrifying event that was taking place on the television screen only mildly distracted me from the pain.

Eating only macrobiotic foods, my latest attempt at a healthy lifestyle, left me very thin and dangerously anemic, lacking the iron and protein my body needed. The muscle around my heart became inflamed, an extremely painful condition that eventually went away with medication. My doctor reprimanded me for my poor health, instructing me to go home and eat spinach and liver. She also referred me to a heart specialist who gave me an EKG and anti-depressants. He told me that my heart would be fine if I got rid of the stress.

"No problem," I mumbled as I walked out.

The number of nights I spent waiting for the phone to ring or for Glen's car to pull into the driveway, was too high to count. Two or three times per week would be a fair estimate. The next day was spent trying to arouse him by phone from my office, or in person on the weekends. I covered for him with his employer, children, ex-wife, and friends. Once we were married, we joined forces in my contracting business, that being one of the reasons for getting married. At the time I thought it might help him become more responsible. We worked well together during the day, with very few conflicts and a well-balanced workload. Most of our problems revolved around his after-hour pastimes, that and dealing with his ex, my ex, five kids, and one bathroom every damn weekend.

Glen promised he would change when he asked me to marry him, and he continued to promise that many times over the years. I don't know why I held on with so many reasons to let go, but I did. The embarrassment I felt each time the police called me to bring him home left me feeling angry and ashamed. Arrested several times for Driving Under the Influence, he posed a clear danger to himself and others. I often accompanied him on his evenings out, mainly to ensure that he made it home.

My kids, in turn, started going out and getting in trouble while I was babysitting my husband. I am forever grateful that neither of them did anything fatal or terribly illegal. I did my best to be a good mother and a good wife, but it seemed like I was failing at both. Life felt overwhelming, with a difficult business to run, two spirited teenagers, and yet another useless husband.

When a person, especially a wife, hangs her head and keeps her mouth shut while she is being mistreated, it's like giving permission to her abuser to continue the behavior. It seemed normal to me that I should be in charge of all responsibilities; that was how I lived for as long as I could remember. Taking care of others and asking little for myself was a product of low self-esteem, not any form of benevolence or altruism. Always being nice and not standing up for myself were acts of cowardice that I recognized, yet I didn't want to admit to another failed marriage. In addition, my kids' teachers had finally stopped blaming any and all of their misdemeanors on the fact that I was a single parent.

The depression I tried to hide made me feel sure that I was going crazy. I thought constantly about committing suicide, but such a selfish act on my part would have destroyed my children; their lives were already hard enough, thanks to me. Nearly all of my friends and several of Glen's friends knew how unhappy I was, even though I usually defended my husband when they pointed out his faults. His friends admired me for being such a good wife, most of them having already lost their own.

After too many years in another bogus marriage, despondent and disheartened, I wound up in another man's arms. Kevin was fifteen years older than me, divorced with four grown children. We met on my fortieth birthday, at Glen's favorite bar. At first our flirtation was innocent, one I thought might get my husband's attention. An electrical contractor that our company hired whenever we had the need, Kevin often spent time with Glen because they worked on the same projects. He approached me at lunch one day while I was finalizing a bid. When he asked if he could pay for my lunch, I shrugged and said, "It's your money."

He cocked his head, raising one well-defined eyebrow, and smiled as he responded, "Well, it was your money first, so you might as well take me up on my offer."

Later that day, after hearing the news that my company was awarded the contract, our largest one to date, Kevin stopped by my office with a bottle of wine to celebrate. He knew that Glen was already celebrating at a downtown bar. From then on, there was nothing he wouldn't do, no chance he wouldn't take, to be with me. Having the attention of such a handsome older man lifted my confidence at first, but my spirit suffered and I soon felt consumed by guilt. I wasn't in love with this man, but I needed someone to confirm that I was alive, worthy of love and attention.

Colleen lived in another state and was shocked when I told her about my affair—so unlike me. I had felt too humiliated to tell her how bad things were with Glen, but I felt the need to confess my outrageous sin to someone. Best friends can support your conscience and help heal your spirit; after my call, she decided to pay me a visit. When she saw first-hand how abusive Glen could be when he drank too much, she begged me to leave him. I promised I would, just as soon as I figured out how. I didn't plan to bid on another contract, but I had an obligation, both legal and moral, to finish the ones I had. After Colleen's visit I stopped seeing Kevin, not only because of the guilt, but because I realized that he was so much like Glen.

My children were now adults, so I decided the time was right to formulate an escape plan. Dawn had left home three years earlier, right after she graduated from high school, having refused to register at any of the colleges that accepted her application, including MIT. I had toiled over the financial aid forms, paid the application fees, and taken her to visit campuses. For years I regretted not forcing her into my car and dropping her off at the admissions office. I felt nearly as helpless at dealing with my teenagers as I was at dealing with men.

Dawn's father had taken her to Europe as her high school graduation present. His gifts of no rules and high living made normal life seem dull, so she had decided to wait a year before going to college. She moved to Florida to work for her father and ended up living with friends who had no plans at all. Even though Paul had split with Elsie long ago, he seemed to be a bigger jerk than ever, one that gave his daughter a credit card to keep her out of his hair. He was busy dating a flight attendant and working on his golf game.

It broke my heart to see my beautiful daughter so lost. No one, including Dawn, knew she was pregnant when she moved away, and her father ignored the fact that she gained so much weight while she was working for him. She returned home eight months later to arrange an adoption for her baby. Nine months pregnant, she drove herself twelve hundred miles in a twenty-year-old Mustang, to a birthing center in Vermont to select her baby's parents. She stayed with a friend who lived two miles away from my house, until her baby boy was born. She didn't tell me she was nearby until the ordeal was over, then confessed in tears and shame.

I held her in my arms and told her that I had never been more proud of her. I was in awe of her bravery and strength, but I felt terrible that she hadn't asked for my help. She always insisted that "kids shouldn't have kids," and she knew she wasn't ready to raise a child. She also knew that I would have tried to take on more responsibilities, even though I couldn't handle the ones I already had.

PJ came to me when he heard the rumor. "What's going on, Mom? Did Dawn really have a kid? Man, what a bummer; I don't even get to know him." He never mentioned him again, not even to Dawn, which probably made her feel even worse about herself. I called Paul to let him know he had a grandson. He never mentioned him again, either.

Unlike his sister, my son insisted on going to college even though he had never been studious or even serious about school. His buddies were going, and he didn't want to miss out on all that partying. By now the word meant actual parties—lots of kids, beer...sex, drugs, rock and roll. I tried to believe that my kids would never do drugs, but it was the eighties and who didn't.

When I dropped Paul Jr. off at his campus, he laughed and said, "I'm going to screw more people than the IRS."

"Oh, you think so Hotshot? Well, you'd better keep your grades up or you'll screw yourself out of an education." I gave a little pull on his sleeve as I spoke, then rubbed his shoulder a couple of times to let him know how much I loved him. That gesture had been our code since he turned seven and decided he was too old for affection.

He smiled and said, "Thanks, Mom," and actually gave me a hug before he climbed out of the car. As he sauntered away, he held his hand over his head and waved without looking back. In spite of all those years of turmoil, or maybe because of them, he had developed a great sense of humor and a fearless attitude. Unfortunately, it takes more than humor and spunk to succeed in college and he left the following year. He chose to work in the hospitality industry, and being a talented cook as well as a hard worker, he had no trouble finding a job even without the degree. He soon moved to Colorado to work at a ski resort and continued to party, earning the nickname, "Party On Paul."

Dawn had made some good friends while living in Florida, so she decided to move back there. I'm sure she felt the distance would make it easier to recover from the sadness of giving up her son. No number of miles could put him out of her heart or her mind, but she'd have to wait eighteen years to see him again. Within a year she married a young man named Andy, and was about to give birth to a baby girl. I decided to start another business, this time in Florida so that I could be near my daughter and grandchild.

It has been said that if you give a person enough rope, he might hang himself. After I left, Glen started using all the rope I had given him. He promised to shape up and keep our company running while I got the new business off the ground, and I agreed to come back to help him as soon as I hired someone to run the store I opened.

The store, a glorified gift shop that carried products from my home state, as well as antiques and art, was called *Just Vermont.* I found what looked like a great location, in an exclusive shopping center in Fort Lauderdale. Even though the parking lot was filled with expensive cars and wealthy people, I knew in my heart that the store was a risky idea. At the time however, it seemed like the easiest way to climb out of the giant hole I seemed to have sunken into. Opening the store was something I always wanted to do; I wasn't really planning to return to that hole.

Before I left Vermont, I hired a secretary named Sandy who seemed to have the exact qualities needed to help with my plan. She was quite pretty, easy to be around, and a little loose. In all my years of running the company, I never kept a secretary for more than a few months. It seemed easier to do everything myself so it would get done right. I did my best to teach Sandy how to run the office, knowing full well that she wasn't capable of doing the job. Glen would just have to deal with it. I sent Sandy on errands to the job sites or to pick up inventory for my new venture, while I prepared for my departure. In some ways, my new secretary was working out well. In no time at all she started going out with the guys for drinks. After I left, she not only went out with Glen quite often, she became one of Kevin's conquests as well.

While Sandy's husband was out looking for her one stormy night, he was involved in a head-on collision, killing a nurse, the mother of two small children, on her way home from work. The accident, which happened during the holidays, woke everyone up. From that tragedy, I learned not to mess with other people's lives. Sure, it was their own doing and no one forced them to get together, but I felt like I had set them up. Now I had to live with it. I told Glen over the phone that I'd heard about the accident and his nights out with Sandy.

"It's over between us, Glen. I'm not coming home."

The phone line went dead. He later told me that he ripped the phone out of the wall and broke down in tears. He thought a mutual friend ratted on him, and that was somewhat true. I didn't tell him that the rat was Kevin, who still called me fairly often to report those types of things, probably to make him feel better about himself. I certainly didn't consider him a friend.

Glen called nearly every day and begged for forgiveness. He swore that he'd stop drinking, gambling, and everything else. Having heard those same promises so many times, I turned to ice. When the ice finally shattered, I suffered a major meltdown. Leaving my store unattended, I rushed to my apartment, collapsing in a haze of hysteria and weakness. For days I felt like I was drowning in a pool of regrets; then came denial, and finally acceptance. Cleansed by emotional drainage, I started to feel stronger.

My estranged husband met a young woman named Michelle while he was out drinking one night, less than a month after I told him we were through. He filed for a divorce after she became pregnant. I let him handle the entire situation, never even consulted a lawyer. Glen was fair about splitting the profits and I was simply happy that our marriage was over. It didn't bother me that my company went down the drain, nor did it matter that many of my possessions were lost during the time it took to liquidate. I felt that I was swapping material things for something far more precious. Freedom. I hoped to find peace in solitude; I certainly had not found any peace in partnerships.

My store was doing poorly. It was a wonderful place to spend the day, yet it became obvious very early on that I had a losing proposition on my hands. Having spent over a year searching out the very best artisans and products that Vermont has to offer, fabulous items covered every surface. Interesting artwork lined the walls and attractive displays filled the shelves and windows. However, location is everything and mine turned out not to be a good one. The parking lot had been crawling with Jaguars, BMW's and Mercedes when I rented the space. TGI Friday's was always busy, as were the beauty salons, nail boutiques, and dry cleaners. Across the parking lot sat my store, usually empty. The store was a combination gift shop, antique and art gallery—too big, too diverse, and too comfortable. Customers loved to browse around and visit with me, most of them buying small gifts, maple syrup, or Cabot cheese, but not enough to pay the rent. I knew I'd have to sell the place or close it, chalk it all up to experience.

Although the bottom line was a red one, I enjoyed the process and the people. Now and then a celebrity wandered in, probably a few I didn't recognize. Gene Hackman nearly escaped my notice until he purchased an antique vase one day. On another occasion, Jessica Lange and her son Walker came into the store. She had recently starred in a remake of Cape Fear, which was filmed in the area. The boy's father, Sam Shepard, was my favorite play-write, and Jessica was a popular actress. We chatted for a while since they were the only customers in the store at the time. She seemed pleased that I knew who she was yet didn't act star-struck. She used a credit card to pay for the teddy bear her son chose to keep him company on their long trip, to a ranch in Virginia, I think she said. At the time I wished she had offered me a job, maybe nanny or secretary, anything. I sighed as I watched their long white limousine drive away, wondering why she hadn't spent more of her money in what she called my "fascinating store."

Little could be done to increase the foot traffic in the shopping center, and having had no luck selling the business, I wrote to the group who owned the complex and asked to be released from my rental contract. My sales receipts proved how badly the store was doing. Unable to pay the huge rent that was called for in my lease, the agency had allowed me to pay only the Common Area Maintenance fees. I wasn't able to make a living, even staying open ten hours, seven days per week. Incredible as it seemed, this group of big city lawyers and realtors let me off the hook. Over twenty thousand dollars in back rent was waived. I gratefully accepted the papers they prepared, voiding my lease agreement and allowing me thirty days to vacate.

Now all I needed to do was dispense with two floors of inventory and display cases. Much of the artwork and a few antiques were on consignment, so I returned anything that wasn't already paid for, and sold everything else at cost or less. I made up gift baskets of gourmet food items, toys, and crafts to donate to local charities. I drove down Broward Boulevard handing out bags of Vermont-made tortilla chips, candy, and other food items to anyone who looked needy—a practice I started on my first Christmas in the store. By the end of the thirty days, eighteen hundred square feet of inventory was reduced to one large truckload.

I had purchased a house with the profits I received from the sale of the business and real estate that Glen and I owned together, which meant I had a home and a place to store the unsold goods. And even though it was located in Florida, the property was an excellent investment and a pleasant place to live. It was considered a villa, one of four homes separated by firewalls, surrounded by other like buildings in a perfectly manicured cul-de-sac.

The state of Florida offered warmth and anonymity, but I wasn't sure I'd ever get used to living there. The radiant sunshine and sandy beaches couldn't make up for the steaming humidity, insane traffic, or the sense of being lost in another strange place. But I did have a home there, and I had been offered a well paying job. In addition, my daughter and granddaughter lived only a few hours away.

They were alone now, too. Kate's father turned out to be even more worthless than Dawn's own father. Andy left Dawn to be with a seventeen-year-old coed, shortly after their daughter was born. The girls needed me there, and I needed them. *Plus,* I thought to myself: *How many times can a person go home*?

Chapter 4

Fleeting Emotions

Three failed marriages left me with a heavy heart and a fractured spirit, wallowing in regret for having made such bad choices, for giving in to false and fleeting emotions because of the need to feel loved. As I watched my daughter try to find her way down a similar path, I wondered if she was destined to make the same mistakes.

Colleen scolded me for being so hard on myself. "Stop beating your self up," she said. "Dawn will learn from her mistakes and yours. You need to stop worrying about the past and learn to enjoy life. You've been through hell, my friend. We all make bad choices sometimes. Now, give yourself a break and have some fun."

I agreed to give that a try, knowing it would take time. Having fun comes easily for some people, but for others it has to be learned. There hadn't been a whole lot of fun in my life, especially in childhood when laughter and joy should have been spontaneous. As a teenager, the fear of eternal damnation kept me from having fun lest I commit a mortal sin, or even a venial one, to bring to the confessional on Saturday morning. Marrying at eighteen and becoming a mother at nineteen hadn't left much time for fun either, especially with a husband who only cared about his own happiness.

I felt lucky to have a friend who knew me and understood. She had flown in from Boston to acquire her yearly tan and to spend New Year's Eve with me. We decided to go out for a few drinks and listen to some music. Collie was the one special friend that I could tell anything to and hear anything from. While we were talking, she pointed out that all the men in my life had chosen me, never the other way around. I assured her that I would try not to let that happen again.

After closing my store, I took a part-time job doing data entry for a small electronics company in Broward County. The experience gained from running my own businesses proved to be very helpful to my new bosses, both of whom possessed the business sense of a weasel. The two former drug dealers had bought out a failing company, and somehow managed to turn it around by working hard, taking chances, and by having a certain amount of dumb luck. When they saw how easily I organized my office and finished my work, they offered me a full-time management position at a much higher salary.

Within a few months I was running the business, leaving the partners free to pursue other interests. They set about trying to outspend each other. Ted sailed off to the Bahamas for fun in the sun, while Jeremy ordered a sexy young wife from Brazil. When Ted found out that Jeremy paid for his fiancée's boob job with a company check, he questioned why his partner hadn't just ordered someone better endowed, and then went out and bought a bigger boat. And so it went. I found their antics amusing, not bothered in the least by anything they chose to do. I just worked there.

For my birthday that year, Joe and Diane sent me a round trip ticket to spend the holidays with them in Connecticut. We had become friends when I worked as a waitress, the two of them often eating in the restaurant, always sitting in my station when they came in. Joe handled my divorce from Paul while Diane provided emotional support, her sarcastic humor helping me stay sane. She was quite happy that I was on my own again, not having been terribly impressed with the men in my life.

During my visit, Joe invited an old friend to join us for dinner, hoping somehow to persuade me to move back to New England. The guest was Joe's best friend, Dominic. He and I dated briefly after my first divorce, but the flame we once shared had burned out long ago. It was good to see him and to reaffirm that I made at least one good decision in my life—the decision to break up with him. He hadn't wanted to bother with my children, and a divorcee just wasn't acceptable to his old school, Italian-Catholic parents. Dominic was now living with and caring for his widowed mother. I felt like I had dodged a missile.

I returned to my job in Florida and to the anonymous life I had assumed. In my workaholic fashion, it didn't matter whether I liked my work as long as there was plenty to do. I was making great money and enjoying a comfortable lifestyle. My children seemed happy, and even though I missed them, it felt good that I could help them out financially and provide a nice place to stay when they came to visit, which they did quite often.

Paul Jr. was settled in his new life, managing a restaurant in Colorado and dating a magnificent young woman from Tulsa who would eventually become my daughter-in-law. Dawn, now divorced, had decided to move back to Vermont with my darling little granddaughter. I had moved to Florida to get away from Glen, and because Dawn and Kate were there. Now they were gone, leaving me feeling somewhat abandoned, but I made the best of it.

My social life was fairly interesting thanks to a friend from work. Nancy was a gourmet cook and a fabulous hostess. She and her husband, Gino, loved having parties—big ones, with lots of great food and plenty of booze. They knew how to enjoy life, something that I was still working on. The handsome couple became my mentors in the quest for a happy and carefree existence.

With their encouragement, I allowed another man to come into my life. Taylor was a friend of my bosses. He and I had known each other since I started my job two years earlier. At work he was known as "the consultant." Called in whenever the company needed any type of program implemented, Taylor seemed capable of solving nearly any problem. My bosses relied on him to help make the changes needed for their growing company. He probably could have been making a huge salary and driving an expensive car, had he been the least bit interested in either of those things. Instead, he drove an old red minivan, bleached a brownish pink by the ruthless Florida sun, its back crammed full with file boxes—an office on wheels. He bartered much of his work. For what, I wasn't sure.

The first time I saw Taylor, he was coming up the stairs toward my office, two steps at a time. He wore scuffed leather boat shoes and his baggy jeans showed a good deal of wear. On the front of his T-shirt was a picture of a tree holding a sign that said, "Save the humans." He was in his mid thirties, tall and thin, dark complexioned, with brown eyes and hair. His British-Canadian accent exuded an air of confidence. I found his gentle demeanor and quick wit appealing and we became fast friends, often finding ourselves at the same social events on invitation from Nancy.

One day Taylor overheard me making arrangements to take a friend's daughter to see a movie, and he expressed an interest in going. It seemed a bit odd that he would want to watch *The Little Mermaid*, but I didn't mind having some adult company. He met us at the movie, a matinee. Afterwards, we both went to the party that was taking place at Nancy and Gino's house, and I delivered the little girl to her parents who were at the same gathering. Gino insisted that the two of us stay for a dip in the hot tub, after everyone else went home.

Taylor walked me to my car when we left, pecked me on the cheek, and told me that he'd had a splendid time. When our cars stopped at a traffic light to turn our separate ways, I threw him a kiss and waved. I had no idea what that gesture would do to his head. He had massaged my feet in the hot tub after one of them floated near him. Feeling little inhibition after several glasses of wine, I hadn't objected. Light fun, nothing serious; the way friends are with each other. Or so I thought. I didn't realize that my friend was looking for a little more than friendship.

I knew Taylor had been keeping an eye on me, but I hadn't taken him all that seriously. We worked together often, always talking and joking around. He knew about my marriages, my children, and my friends. When he quipped that women didn't seem to be interested in him, I jokingly offered to let him practice on me. He watched and waited, hoping that I wouldn't fall for anyone else. Both of my bosses were single since Jeremy returned his mail-order bride to South America after catching her with the pool boy, but they were playboys and I wasn't interested in playing. Ted and Jeremy praised me often and compensated me well. I repaid their generosity and trust by working harder than anyone should. Even on Saturdays, I worked at least six hours, shopped for food, and then went home to start my short weekend.

One Saturday afternoon, the day before Valentine's Day, as I was putting away my groceries, a splash of color caught my eye. On the patio table outside my kitchen window, sat a large red pottery vase containing a generous bouquet of assorted flowers. I walked outside, wondering who might have brought me flowers. Thinking it must be a gift from Nancy, I smiled as I opened the card. I blinked as I read: "*Happy Valentine's Day! Love, Taylor.*"

My heart fluttered, actually fluttered, as I picked up the heavy vase. *Nineteen-year-old hearts flutter, not forty-five year-old hearts,* I thought to myself. It took at least an hour to get over the shock and call to thank him.

"You're quite welcome," he replied. "I wanted to show you how much I appreciate all your help with the new system. It was a real bear; I couldn't have done it without you. You're not paid nearly what you deserve."

"This is true," I joked, even though I didn't agree.

After we hung up, I walked around with a smile on my face for hours. He was too young, but it felt good to smile. My job was difficult and demanding, made worse by working too hard and taking things too seriously. Work hard, play hard, work harder. I didn't realize it was a disease.

Taylor finished the current project at my office and then left to spend some time with his family in Toronto. It seemed strange that I missed him so much; we were just friends after all. A couple of times while he was away, I called him from work to discuss small problems. He also called me several times to see how things were going or to talk to one of the guys, always calling my line instead of one of theirs. Ted and Jeremy continued to entertain us with their lavish lifestyles and inane business ventures. They had recently started a pyramid scheme, selling designer vitamins and over-priced bodybuilding formulas.

When Taylor came back to town, he called and asked if we could get together. Still thinking of him as a platonic friend, I invited him over for tacos. He stood in the kitchen talking to me while I cooked, and for the first time, his presence made me nervous. I emptied an entire package of seasoning into the half recipe of meat and onions. The tacos tasted terrible. We laughed about the mistake as we added salsa to the mix and piled on cheese, lettuce, and tomatoes.

After we ate, Taylor told me that he composed a poem for me while he was away. The poem was beautifully written, about me being in my autumn and him in summer's heat. It made me laugh and I hugged him. He told me that he would feel proud if I'd agree to become his girlfriend. I had never heard anything so old-fashioned and romantic. In spite of my better judgment, I told him that I would consider it. Now *he* was nervous, and he kissed me good night as though I might break, patting me gently on the back as he gave me a short hug.

He will definitely need more practice, I thought as he opened the door to leave.

Over the next two weeks, we met for lunch a few times and talked on the phone nearly every day. Our only official date was dinner and an Eagles concert, after which Taylor asked me whether I had made up my mind. I hadn't. The following day, he called to ask if he could come over on Saturday night. *Casablanca* was playing on television and we were both Bogart fans. Taylor didn't drink alcohol, but he smoked some pot while I sipped my wine. The night turned out to be great fun, filled with laughter, conversation, and eventually, sex.

The next morning we went to breakfast together. It felt strange being with him. I was very aware of our age difference, something that had never been an issue when we were just friends. I tried to convince myself it was just a fling, a fleeting emotion. But I had known this guy for nearly two years, and so far I hadn't found anything other than his age and a seemingly harmless drug habit, that I didn't like about him. He had no ex-wife, no phobias, no baggage at all, that I could see.

For the next few weeks we watched together in horror as the Waco travesty took place, growing closer as the rest of the world was seemingly going crazy. We spoke out against NAFTA and GATT, and the many other unfair policies in our country and throughout the world, astonished that none of our acquaintances seemed to care about anything other than having a good time and earning a decent paycheck. We discussed politics and religion, family and traveling. He and I shared a similar taste in music, we liked watching the same shows, and we enjoyed spending time together. I had been a recluse for the most part, and Taylor seemed to have more friends than Elvis. He played several musical instruments, jamming often with fellow musicians. I usually stayed home, savoring my solitude, seldom accepting his invitations to join him. Staying out late would have made it harder for me to be the first one at work in the morning.

Somehow Taylor moved in with me before I really knew what was happening. He kept his apartment for several months, making his invasion unapparent at first. His belongings soon filled a previously un-used closet. Those months of watching me, and becoming friends with me, had been carefully calculated. Slowly and slyly, another man made his way into my heart. And once again, I allowed that to happen with little resistance.

He started calling me at work more often, sometimes several times in one day, and it wasn't work related. He'd ask when I'd be home and acted agitated when I made other plans, whether I was working late or spending time with Nancy. At first it seemed sort of nice that someone cared where I was and what I was doing, but I soon began to feel smothered. When I told him that I didn't want to have to account for my every move, he assured me that he was only showing how much he cared. He didn't think it should bother me that he wanted to spend all his time with me. But it did.

One evening, a few months after he gave up his apartment and moved into my villa, Taylor greeted me at the door when I came home from work. The house looked neater than usual, much of his clutter moved out of sight. He had picked up some sushi and bought a bottle of my favorite wine. I was delighted and surprised, as he didn't usually provide dinner or help with the household chores. After we ate, he poured me a second glass of wine. I started to get suspicious when he cleared the table, something he never did unless I asked him to. When he came out of the kitchen, I had relocated to the sofa. He sat down beside me, took my hand, and kissed me. The look on his face told me something was coming even before he spoke.

"Rose, my love, we need to talk. I know you don't think it's necessary for us to be married, but it truly is. My parents are terribly concerned about us living together without the benefits of marriage. You are the woman I intend to spend my life with, and I simply do not feel that we can be in a committed relationship unless we get married. This isn't proper; it's, well, it's living in sin."

Oh, no, I thought, *here we go again. Who is this, Charles reincarnated*?

I sighed and blew out a deep breath as I started to speak. "Taylor, why did you move in here without telling me that you expected me to marry you? I didn't ask you to move in, and you didn't ask if you could move in; you just did. Maybe I shouldn't have let that happen, but once you were here, I guess I thought it would be okay to live together and help each other. I've been married three times. Three times, for heavens sake! Do you really want to be husband number four? You can't be serious."

"Fourth and final," was his response. "I've already spoken with my pastor and explained to him that one of your husbands died and the other two committed adultery. He offered to give us pre-marital counseling. We can make this work; I know we can. Darling, you do love me, don't you?"

I sat there with my mouth open, staring at him in disbelief. I didn't want another husband. I liked having Taylor as my roommate, for the most part, and I wanted to keep it that way. Even though I actually preferred living alone, I had grown to appreciate his affections and his companionship, and living in South Florida felt safer with a man around. What I didn't appreciate was being manipulated, which was exactly how this felt. I told him that I wasn't ready for such a big step and that I didn't know if I ever would be. He was clearly disappointed, although he said he understood. He hoped I'd change my mind but his parents would simply have to accept things as they were, for now.

Although Taylor agreed to accept my decision not to marry, he continued to make subtle efforts to change my mind. When I asked why he didn't jam with his friends anymore, he told me that he would rather spend his time with me, doing things around our house. He repaired the atrium that had been damaged the previous year during Hurricane Andrew. He built a patio and planted a rose garden beside the new fence that he and some friends installed. He loosened his grip on me, somewhat, and tried not to bother me at work. And when Nancy asked me to go shopping or come to her house for a visit, he no longer objected or insisted on coming along. She commented more than once that he seemed very possessive.

"You'd better watch out for this one, Rosebud," she warned. "Still waters run deep."

"Whatever that means, Nan," I laughed.

I admitted to her that I was a little leery of Taylor's efforts to win my hand, but it certainly did not bother me that he was making repairs. Since he didn't contribute much toward the household expenses, it only seemed fair that he should help with maintenance. As time wore on, he managed to earn my trust through his hard work and eagerness to please me. His parents continued to ask him when we were getting married, and he sometimes joked that they were still on his back. His mother was adamant about her religious beliefs and his father concurred, seemingly to keep her content.

Taylor strived to get closer to Dawn and Kate, always the perfect host when they visited. He taught Kate to play chess, and showed Dawn how to utilize online search engines. When PJ brought his fiancé to meet me, Taylor fawned over Carrie and played golf with PJ, convincing everyone that he was the best thing in the world for me. My children were happy that I wasn't alone, but they both agreed with my decision to stay single. The fact that this guy was more than a dozen years my junior was a little embarrassing, even though my favorite uncle was eighteen years younger than my aunt. Their age difference never seemed odd while I was growing up, but for some reason ours did.

As time drew on, I became more comfortable with Taylor's presence, little by little dropping my guard and slipping into the comfort zone of living as a married couple. Things went on that way for a couple of years. Then he asked again, ring in hand, a family heirloom no less. He insisted that he'd been patient long enough, and that he would absolutely leave the country unless I married him.

By now there didn't seem to be any good reason to refuse him, and even though I wasn't excited about going into another marriage, I agreed to become his wife. We were married in our back yard with sixty friends and relatives present, many of them traveling from as far away as Canada to attend. Nancy catered the affair, somewhat skeptical, but quite happy to run the show. She helped me find the perfect wedding dress, planned the menu, and helped with the floral arrangements. Caught up in the planning, she forgot all about her concerns, guiding me every step of the way down that primrose path. She and Gino were planning to move to Tennessee soon; she wouldn't be around to see what lay at the end of the path.

PJ gave my hand in marriage as much as he didn't want to be there, especially since Carrie couldn't make the trip. My son shares my dislike of crowds, and this was a tough assignment, with so few people he knew. "Only for you, Mom," he told me, "but never again." I promised him, and myself, that this would be the very last time.

Dawn was delighted to be my maid of honor, looking gorgeous, a little worried yet happy for me. Five-year-old Kate made an angelic flower girl, humorously paying far more attention to her audience than to the basket of rose pedals she had been instructed to scatter along the brick path that Taylor carefully built for the occasion. He spent weeks on the project, making sure that every brick was perfectly placed. New sod covered the sun-dried lawn and multi-colored Bougainvillea lined the fence. I was duly impressed.

Colleen traveled to be at my side, even though she told me straight-out that she thought Taylor was too young for me. She had watched me suffer through the last two bad marriages, and she couldn't understand why I would chance another one. Within a few days, however, Taylor won her over with his quirky sense of humor and warm hospitality.

As I was about to follow Kate down the path, I turned to Colleen and whispered, "Wish me luck."

She took my hand and said, "Good luck, Sweetie. Maybe the fourth time's a charm." Her eyes showed concern, as though she could sense the fear that was growing rapidly in my heart as I stepped onto the bricks.

The wedding was beautiful. Everyone feasted on Nancy's outrageous buffet and the meticulously decorated cake that Taylor's mother baked. Exquisitely wrapped gifts were piled on the credenza, and envelopes holding generous checks were tossed in a heart-shaped dish. The evening air smelled of jasmine as guests danced on the lawn to music performed by Taylor's friends. Everything seemed perfect. My fears began to melt like the ice in my vodka and cranberry juice.

Alas, as passionate as Taylor seemed about getting married, once we exchanged our vows all that passion seemed to disappear. He may have decided that once he officially became my husband, he didn't need to try anymore. We spent our four-day honeymoon in a rented cottage beside a lake in northern Florida. My new husband went fishing every day while I sat in the shade reading and enjoying the songbirds. Each evening, he plugged in his laptop just as he did when we were at home. Brushing off my feelings of melancholy, I lit candles, took baths, and pretended to be happy.

On the last day of our honeymoon, I took Taylor's hand and asked him to go for a walk with me. He said he didn't feel like walking, that I should go without him. I told him I was feeling somewhat neglected, that he hadn't done or said anything romantic since we got married.

After giving me a patronizing smile, he shrugged and said, "Marriage isn't a fairy tale, my dear. It's two people spending their life together, in harmony. That should be enough. I love you; that's why I married you. I shouldn't think I'd have to continue proving it, Rose."

Maybe he's right, I thought. *It should be enough to know that the person you're with loves you and wants to share his life with you. Why am I not feeling that? Why do I need more?*

For three or four years, I kept up a good front. I had made my bed, and now I would sleep in it. When Nancy called to see how married life was treating me, I told her that everything was fine. I didn't try to pretend with Colleen; she wouldn't have bought it anyway. Both of us were saddened by the fact that marriage number four already appeared doomed. She never once said, "I told you so."

I worked even harder at my job, and I flew to Vermont every few months to be with my younger sister. Meg was terminally ill with chronic heart and lung problems. Watching her suffer and feeling helpless about living so far away, contributed to the stress that was wearing me down. I started having anxiety attacks, with chest pains so severe that I called 9-1-1 on two occasions. Taylor wasn't there either time. He had started an advertising agency with his friend Marcel and was spending most of his time at Marcel's apartment, which was also their office. The neglect that surfaced during our honeymoon, not only continued, it grew.

Each time the paramedics came, they concluded that I was having a panic attack, instructing me to see a doctor the next day. My HMO health care provider was fond of writing prescriptions. My medicine cabinet soon contained sedatives, anti-depressants, and painkillers, as well as hormone replacement therapy and cholesterol lowering drugs. I didn't take the medications the doctor gave me, nor did I take his advice to stop working so hard. Staying busy helped keep my mind off my problems and my gnawing unhappiness.

One morning, while driving to yet another doctor's visit, a car shot out from a parking lot, slamming into my car and forcing it into the median, knocking me unconscious. The man who witnessed the accident called the police, and he and the man who caused the accident helped me out of my car to safety after I regained consciousness. I had been driving at a moderate speed, in the middle lane of a busy three-lane highway. Everyone seemed amazed that our two cars were the only ones involved in the accident. The other driver was in town visiting his wife's family, driving his mother-in-law's new car. His name was Dr. Conrad Kessler, a dream therapist from Grants Pass, Oregon. He was unable to explain what had happened, or why he hadn't seen my car when he pulled out of the parking lot. I remembered that a large truck passed me on the right just before the accident occurred. Dr. Kessler was cited for Failure To Use Due Caution.

The crash left me feeling shaky, stiff, and hurting all over. Nothing seemed to be broken, so I refused a ride to the hospital in the ambulance that arrived on the scene. I don't remember who called Taylor from the accident, but I do remember that he was too busy to come. He asked a neighbor to give me a ride home. I went to bed and rested for a few days, and then tried to return to my job.

Unable to continue in my managerial position, I worked part time, using braces and ice packs to get through the hours. For over six years I had run the company, gaining the respect and admiration of my bosses and coworkers by working myself nearly to death. Now that I could no longer do the job, their admiration seemed to wane—a huge blow to my ego, what little was left.

The other driver's insurance company paid to repair my car and reimbursed me for the time I lost from work, but my letters and calls asking for help with medical bills were ignored. The ten thousand dollar PIP (personal injury protection) provided by my own auto insurance, was quickly exhausted. And because I no longer worked full time, I wasn't eligible for health insurance through my job. An MRI showed three herniated discs in my back, one broken and pressing on my sciatic nerve. I needed surgery but without insurance, doctors refused to treat me. Sixteen months after the accident, no longer able to work even part-time, and still being ignored by the other driver's insurance company, I agreed to talk with an attorney that my friend Valerie recommended.

I felt sure that Taylor would help more once he knew the extent of my injuries, but I was wrong. He didn't seem interested in how I was coping with the pain, or even how I was paying the bills. The money that he and Marcel earned barely covered their business expenses, according to Taylor. The patronizing lip service he offered soon became little more than an insult added to my injuries, so I stopped asking for help or explanations.

My dying sister was constantly on my mind; and dealing with this insurance mess while I was in so much pain, both physically and mentally, was beyond agonizing. When Meg died, I was unable to fly home and attend her funeral. Her death seemed like the final blow, and the depression that had hovered over my being for so long quickly spun into despair. I became angry at life, at my husband, and at myself. Once I couldn't stand myself anymore, I started taking the prescribed painkillers and anti-depressants. The medications not only eased my pain, they helped me forget what a travesty my life had become, again. Fortunately the pain pills bothered my stomach, so I was forced to use them sparingly.

Dawn called me daily, and PJ once a week or so; their love and friendship the bright spots in my otherwise bleak days. With their support, along with help from my medications, I started to feel better. I passed my time by resting, reading, and selling my treasures online in an attempt to cover the household expenses. One day, as if suddenly remembering that I could, I started to write. At an early age, writing became my way of working through my problems, using pen and paper as therapy during troubled times. Once again I discovered its pleasant power, and started spending more and more time at my computer.

I had recurrent dreams about a hurricane named Darla, which comes on suddenly and wipes out a good share of the hot, humid peninsula that had been my home for over eleven years. Always fascinated with storms, even as a little girl, I had never been afraid of them the way most children are. The noise, wind, and rain offered escape and excitement. I wrote about the storm, some past adventures, and about my life. As soon as my listing chores were completed each day, I'd lose myself to writing for as long as I was alone.

Taylor and Marcel worked strange hours, more normal for them to work, or play, or create, from noon to midnight than anything resembling nine to five. Their customers, whose businesses ranged from car dealerships to online pornographers, seemed impressed by their marketing strategies. I couldn't understand why they weren't making a profit. Any money the two partners managed to make was used for the company's benefit, and *they* were the company. The resentment I felt went completely unnoticed.

The gentleman who slammed into my car that day comforted me after the accident, insisting that accidents happen for a reason and positive that this one would change my life. So far the accident brought only pain and poverty, but I wanted to believe that he was right, that good karma would eventually come around. I had failed at so many things, but I was still learning. So far I learned that insurance companies aren't interested in helping people, that marriage doesn't guarantee happiness, and that friends don't always remain friends once you are no longer helpful or fun to be with.

My attorney warned me that I could be under surveillance and that the insurance company's legal team and doctors would try to disprove my claim. I was deposed, questioned, examined and reexamined until I wanted to run away screaming. My attorney was confident, diligent, and ruthless. His secretary treated me with kindness and respect, without which I would have given up. At one point the insurance company requested mediation and offered me a paltry settlement, barely enough to cover surgery and legal fees. Their attorney acted even more smug and condescending than usual; soon the reason became clear. I'd been videotaped picking up palm fronds on my front lawn; she accused me of faking my injuries.

I had asked Taylor at least a dozen times to "please clean up the lawn," which he always promised he'd do *later*. I had finally given up on him, strapped on my back brace, took some pain pills, and got the job done. I vaguely remembered a white van parked across the street. Taylor became outraged when he found out that my act of defiance had been caught on tape. He didn't apologize for his indolence, just reprimanded me for doing something so "bloody stupid." I felt despondent, hurt by my husband's criticism and irate that I had been accused of lying. There was nothing fake about my pain or my injuries. I wasn't shown the video, but my face likely showed the pain I was in that day.

My lawyer advised me not to settle. The MRI proved my injuries, my witness was reliable, and we had a solid case. If the insurance company really thought I was faking, they wouldn't have offered me anything. I agreed, determined to stay strong and hold out for a decent settlement. No amount of money would change how things were with Taylor and me, but I needed surgery and a way to get my life together. I started sleeping in the guest room. Sleeping alone was less painful and it made Taylor's comings and goings less obtrusive. He accepted the arrangement with little discussion, still annoyed with me for what he saw as blowing my chance for a settlement.

Chapter 5

Seaside Surprise

After my call to Claire, the kind no one ever gets used to making or receiving, I sat staring out the window at the rain. A blue jay landed on the hedge, then stayed perched there in the rain as if his wings were too heavy with water to allow him to fly, his crest slicked back like the hair of a New Jersey wise guy. Suddenly he shook with a determined wave of his crest, which reappeared as the rain flew off his head like sweat off a singer. Soon he was out of sight, and I thought of him as my brother flying to heaven to be with our people who had gone there before him. Slowly rising from my chair, I went to the kitchen to make myself a cup of tea. I would try to stop shaking before I called my brother Jonathan. Claire would call Mary, Mary would call Earl, and so on.

The news of my brother's death came as a complete shock to all of us. I had talked to him just a few days ago; he wasn't feeling well, said he thought he had the flu. It didn't seem possible that he was gone. He and I had always kept in touch, usually by phone, and we sent each other gifts occasionally. Since he showed no interest in visiting me or in having me visit him, I had left him to himself and the family he had acquired. Larry's life sounded somewhat complicated, not unusual for my brother. Definitely a unique character, he always drove around in some boat-size car, usually a Cadillac, because he said it made him feel classy. I'd helped him out of a few scrapes over the years, even gave him a job when I had my contracting business. He moved to Florida shortly before I did, to some remote area several hours away from me.

According to his attorney, Larry had lived in a mobile home for many years, caring for his late wife's mentally challenged sister, Trudy. He had promised Loretta when she was dying that he would provide for her sister. After Larry's death, Trudy was placed in a nursing home, and from what the nurse told me, she had already forgotten her brother-in-law. I decided to visit her because the nursing home was near the airport where I landed. It was a wasted visit, but I felt sure Larry would have wanted me to go. As if I wasn't depressed enough, I could picture myself there, in one of those beds or a wheelchair. I didn't stay long after talking to the nurse and saying hello to the stranger who had lived with my brother for over ten years. I wondered if she was the reason Larry never invited me to visit.

That night I stayed at a small bed and breakfast, one I'd seen advertised in a newspaper while I was waiting for a taxi. The room had a gingerbread feel, like a cottage in the Swiss Alps where Heidi might have slept. Crystal wind chimes hung from the roof of the balcony outside my room. I sat out late into the night listening to the tinkling of the chimes and the roar of the ocean as the waves hit the breakwater. I fought the urge to walk to the beach, venturing out alone in a strange place at night too risky even for me; plus, the painkillers were starting to wear off. I finally made myself get ready for bed, leaving the French doors open so that I could hear the chimes and feel the breeze.

I woke early and left before breakfast was served, having decided to walk to the beach and have coffee and a muffin at an ocean side café I spotted the night before. The air felt unusually brisk, unlike the humid blast of hot air I had grown used to in South Florida. Living several miles west of the ocean, and with no pool or canal close enough to enhance a breeze, the humidity was extreme. Even here, the day would soon turn hot, I figured. I wasn't looking forward to the heat or to the meeting with Larry's lawyer, but at least I could enjoy my morning.

The smell of salt water and seaweed hit me even before the ocean came into view. The smell reminded me of the Maine coast where Glen stayed when he was on a contract there, the year before we were married. He had rented a cottage less than a mile from the ocean so I walked to the beach every day while he worked, having taken a short vacation while the kids were at camp. I remembered the night that he and I were listening to a local band, when a woman named Joyce approached us. Glen swore he'd never been with her, except as friends during the previous summer; the summer that his kids stayed with me while their mother was in the hospital. Glen's kids annoyed my kids so badly that I let Dawn and PJ fly to Tampa, to visit their Aunt Lilly who had recently moved there. Paul Sr. was in Paris at the time, with yet another new love. Men.

Water under the bridge—the memories evaporated as soon as I saw the ocean. I took a deep, sensual breath of salty-smelling air as I walked slowly toward the café. I sat at a flimsy plastic table weighted down with huge chunks of coral, resting my feet on one of them, with my hands in my sweatshirt pockets while I waited for my coffee. The waitress placed a basket of hot rolls on the table so I didn't order anything else. She left a check for $1.34 after she poured my second cup of coffee. I wondered how they stayed in business; maybe the lunch and dinner crowd was where they made their money. I tucked two singles under the basket and took an extra roll for my walk on the beach, throwing pieces to the shore birds as I walked.

Several sailboats were just beyond the sandbar, and a huge tanker looked small in the distance. At water's edge a young couple attempted to launch their catamaran, a difficult task in the threatening wind. Determined to enjoy my first walk on the beach since before my accident, I ignored the sand that gently whipped my face as I walked. I thought about Taylor and how much he disliked the beach. I couldn't fathom why it held no magic for him; it was the only thing I ever really liked about Florida. Not a sun worshiper, I loved sitting on the beach at sundown until the tide reached my feet, quietly persuading me to go home.

Taylor was too busy to come with me this weekend. The Miami Dolphins had a pre-season game on Sunday and he promised some friends that he would watch the game with them. I asked if he wanted to come with me even though I knew he wouldn't, somewhat relieved that he turned me down but wishing there was someone to help me.

After walking for less than an hour, the pain from my back started its familiar path down my left leg. I sat on the sand and rested for a few minutes before walking back to my room to gather my belongings and head to my appointment. When I entered the inn, the owners, an old German couple, fat and happy as could be, were cleaning up the breakfast room. They invited me to sit and have my complimentary breakfast. After explaining that I had an appointment, I told them how much I enjoyed their inn and that I'd try to come back for a visit before I left town. My brother's death had come up in response to their questions when I checked in. Their kindness seemed genuine as they expressed sorrow for my loss, handing me a container of apple strudel to take with me. August carried my suitcase to the taxi his wife, Greta called when I checked out.

Larry's attorney, Mr. Minton, had a shock of white hair and appeared to be in quite a hurry, probably late for court or something equally important. After a brief introduction and his apologies for having to rush off, he left me with his associate, Attorney Benjamin Carmichael.

"Call me Ben," the man said as he extended his hand. His voice was soft yet distinct, no-nonsense. He seemed slightly embarrassed by the elderly attorney's introduction, which included an announcement that Ben, although an associate with the firm for only three years, was already in line for a partnership. Mr. Minton was clearly fond of his younger associate, assuring me that I would be in good hands.

The clock neared noon by the time we completed the paperwork, which consisted mainly of probate documents and insurance forms. A simple will named me executor, listing Larry's home as his only asset, and requesting that proceeds from the property sale be used for Trudy's care. I would need to sell the place, which was deemed a seaside property even though it sat nearly a mile inland.

Ben offered to drive me there; it was near some land he had looked at when he first moved down from New York. No rental cars had been available at the airport in Fort Myers; I hadn't thought to reserve one. My brother's car was likely parked in his driveway, but who knew what condition it was in. After Ben assured me that I was his only appointment that day, and not knowing the area, I accepted his offer. He loaded my things into his Land Rover, and then held the passenger door open.

As I took in the new car smell, I wondered why this gentleman was being so kind, and why Mr. Minton had seemingly tried to impress me. My brother was far from rich; I guessed they just felt sorry for me.

Ben stopped at a deli along the way, suggesting that I stay in the car and pick out some music for the ride. I was surprised to find a *Simply Red* CD, an Irish band that I really liked and seldom heard. I placed the disk in the slot and adjusted the volume as Ben placed two large bags of groceries behind his seat. I noticed a bottle of wine in one of the bags. He was wearing a wedding band, so I figured he'd bought things to take home later. I thanked him for the water and sandwich he handed me, and then sat back to enjoy the ride. The car's stereo system was awesome, the sound crisp but not tinny, and notes I hadn't heard before were coming through. Ben complimented my music choice, eating his sandwich with some chips as he drove.

We headed south, with the sea in view part of the way. I couldn't remember enjoying a ride more, comfortable with both the vehicle and the driver. This man certainly didn't seem to be your typical yuppie lawyer. No cell phone, and he left his briefcase on his desk. I pegged him as a few years younger than me, or maybe just in better shape. Medium height, rugged build, his dark blond hair graying at the temples and in need of a trim. He wore jeans and a polo shirt, and his denim jacket was tossed across the back seat. I felt relieved that he offered me a ride. Larry's property was nearly an hour's travel, and I doubted that I would have found it on my own. The drive would have been difficult for me even if I knew the way; I hardly ever got behind the wheel of a car anymore.

When I saw the place, I wished I had come alone. Larry told me that he had problems with his legs and feet, but I never knew how serious his condition was. Obviously he had been unable to care for his place, and evidently couldn't afford help. His lawn tractor was parked near the shed, in grass so high that you couldn't see the tires. Several junk cars sat within sight of the driveway, and everything from broken furniture to car parts and tires were piled up behind the shed. An overflowing trash-can was tipped over near the door, perhaps with the help of a neighborhood dog.

I tried to avoid Ben's eyes, hoping that my face didn't show the chagrin I was feeling, all the while ashamed of myself for being embarrassed by my brother's circumstances. Having been here before, Ben showed no reaction. His elbow brushed my shoulder as he walked past me with both bags of groceries in his arms. Realizing I held the keys, I followed slowly as I surveyed the shambles that my brother had called home.

Inside looked even worse than the outside, very messy and with a strong musty odor. The living room resembled a crowded thrift shop where no one ever puts anything away. A relatively new portable television sat atop an older cabinet model, a rabbit-ear antenna balanced on the edge of the top set. Ashtrays and empty coffee mugs littered the coffee table, rings visible from many more.

Larry hadn't told me that he'd been using a wheel chair, which now sat folded up against a wall. Dirty dishes filled the sink and covered much of the kitchen counter, and spots dotted the floor from spills that my brother had been unable to clean. I sighed as I pictured him living here. The last time we spoke on the phone, he had called Social Services to care for his sister-in-law. The healthcare worker that came offered to take him to the clinic, but he had refused to go. When I called again two days later, there was no answer. He had suffered a stroke, caused by a blood clot in his leg. He managed to call 9-1-1, but he died within hours after reaching the hospital.

Ben and I set to work cleaning up the debris off the floor —old newspapers, empty cigarette cartons, junk mail, and candy wrappers. I filled the sink with hot soapy water to cover the dirty dishes, and wiped off counters as Ben carried the trash outside. We didn't say much as we worked. As I cleaned off the shelves in the refrigerator and put away the groceries, I thanked Ben for buying food.

He said, "Don't mention it," as he slumped down onto the overstuffed chair that he'd just cleaned off.

I felt overwhelmed. *How could Larry have lived like this and kept it from me?* I noticed Ben looking at me, which prompted me to speak. "He wasn't that much older than me. I can't believe he was in such bad shape. I could have helped him more, and I should have." I managed not to cry, determined not to appear even more needy or vulnerable.

Ben told me that he'd known my brother for over two years. They met when Ben looked at some land a mile or so down the road. He'd stopped to ask directions while Larry was working on his lawn mower. He asked my brother what had happened to his foot, after noticing his limp as he walked toward the road. Larry told Ben that he hurt his foot when he worked at the pepper cannery, over near Okeechobee. Larry's foreman told him that he wouldn't be able to get worker's compensation, because the accident was his own fault. Larry hadn't even applied, and he got laid off when the cannery cut back. After that, he mowed lawns and fixed lawn mowers. Ben suggested that he call Mr. Minton at the law firm, that he might be able to file a claim even though it had been three years. Four years was the limit.

Ben had recently returned from moving his wife's belongings to Long Island. He hadn't bought the land near my brother's place because *she* didn't like Florida; *he* didn't like Long Island. Mr. Minton informed him of Larry's death when he returned to work. The insurance company had finally offered a small settlement and Larry accepted their offer just before he died, surprised that he was getting anything at all. The proceeds had already been deposited in my brother's account.

"Fat good it will do him now." Then I quickly added, "Damn insurance companies. It was good of you to help him. Thank you."

I took a deep breath then decided out loud to go outside and try to start the old black Lincoln that was parked next to the trailer. I would drive to a store tomorrow to get some cleaning supplies, and maybe some new curtains to replace the haggard-looking ones that were hanging over the windows. I regretted that I hadn't visited Larry and helped him out while he was still alive. I needed to put this place on the market, but it would need some cleaning and a bit of fixing up before that could happen; maybe I would be out of here by Monday. As I was thinking about how to accomplish what needed to be done within two days, it started to rain.

My brother's car wouldn't start. Ben had jumper cables, so he drove his Land Rover around to the front of the old car. He thought it might have a dead battery from being parked so long, but it proved to have far more problems than that. A large, dried pool of transmission fluid stained the ground underneath the car, and whatever gas was in the tank had dried up long ago. The shifter was stuck in reverse. I guessed I wouldn't be driving to the store anytime soon. Ben insisted that he had nothing better to do and would spend the night. He would drive me to town the next morning and I could rent a car, or he could come back and get me in a few days. The rain was coming harder now, and there didn't seem to be much sense in discussion.

After we dried off, I opened some cupboards to see what I could make for dinner. I found a package of egg noodles, canned vegetables and sardines, a small bag of flour, a few spices, and some instant coffee. I started to panic thinking about having to drink instant coffee in the morning, but then remembered that Ben had bought a small bag of ground coffee. It felt foolish to be worried about coffee when I had such a mess to clean, but my morning coffee was one of the few things I still enjoyed in life. Thanks to Ben, there was also milk for my coffee, along with the other staples he had purchased. Of course he knew what we would find, which was why he stopped for groceries.

We had noticed carrots, onions, and squash in my brother's garden as we drove up, both of us expressing surprise that he had a garden. I wondered if a neighbor had lent a hand, or maybe his sister-in-law, Trudy. She seemed too feeble-minded during our visit to be much of a gardener, but I supposed she could have been. A chicken wire fence had been constructed around the small patch of earth, probably to keep out the wildlife.

"Well, let's see." I let out a heavy sigh, holding the cupboard doors open as though I were talking to the cans on the shelf. "I could make Pasta Prima-Verde Alfredo; it's one of my specialties. What do you think about that?"

Ben said, "Sounds great. And we have wine."

While he walked outside to see what could be salvaged from the garden, I filled a large pan with water. Revere Ware. I smiled remembering Larry bragging about his find about a year ago—a full set of pots and pans for forty-nine bucks at Target. All of the pans, dishes, and canned goods were on the lower shelves with the upper shelves mainly empty. My brother must have struggled to get around this place in a wheel chair. I felt my eyes water again, and then changed my focus to preparing a meal.

While I cleaned and cut the vegetables, Ben opened a few windows and tightened the screens. An air conditioner sat in one of the windows, but it made such a racket when he tried it that he quickly turned it off. The rain was spitting through the open windows and slapping the ones that were still closed. Ben had gotten drenched in the garden, which had slowly turned into a giant mud puddle. I laughed while I watched him from the kitchen window, sort of dancing around in the rain looking for things to harvest, seemingly unaware that his performance was providing a diversion from thoughts of my brother's hardships.

He had smiled when he put the dirty vegetables in the sink. "You shouldn't laugh at the hired hand," he scolded, touching the tip of my nose with his wet, dirty finger.

I had wiped the dirt off with my sleeve and went on chopping, amused by his comment and surprised by his touch.

After tightening the screens, Ben walked past me into the bathroom. It took me a while to realize that he was scrubbing the sink and toilet, turning my slight embarrassment to awe. I had never seen any of my husbands or boyfriends clean a bathroom, or any other room for that matter. My son was raised differently, and I knew how much my daughter-in-law appreciated the fact that her husband knew how to cook, clean, and do laundry. A mother's job is to teach her children how to survive, how to get along on their own. I felt I had been a good mother and a good teacher, for the most part. I hadn't set such a great example when it came to staying married, but I had proven over and over again that a person could survive through periods of misery.

By the time dinner was ready, the rain was pounding down hard on the tin roof, and the wind had picked up again. Ben poured us each a glass of wine to have with our pasta, which, though simple, tasted like a gourmet dinner. I hadn't realized how hungry I was until I started eating and didn't stop, nor did Ben. Our meal was largely silent, except for the sounds of forks against the plates and occasional expressions of enjoyment.

Ben let out a small burp after he finished, then chuckled. "Compliments to the chef."

Having so many brothers, and a son who thought all bodily noises were hilarious, Ben's compliment made me feel even more comfortable with him.

"It wouldn't have been nearly as tasty without those fresh veggies you harvested. That was kind of like dancing for your supper," I observed with a smile.

After we picked up the dishes, Ben poured us each another glass of wine and then switched on the television. The picture didn't let us see much except lines, but we could hear the warnings loud and clear.

"A major hurricane has just ripped through Cuba and is rapidly approaching the gulf coast of Florida. The Keys are already experiencing 125 mile-per-hour winds—boats are being tossed about like leaves!"

How could we have missed this, I wondered. I guess, when living in hurricane country, you should always keep a radio on. We had listened to music all the way here, and I hadn't had a television on in days. We watched with our mouths open as the reporter shouted the words ...No, I must have heard wrong. He repeated the warning; Hurricane Darla was about to come ashore!

"Holy Shit!" Ben yelled as he jumped up. "We'd better get some of that trash picked up before this gets any worse. We don't need things flying through the windows. I can't believe this. I watched the weather last night; they were talking about a small tropical storm."

I felt paralyzed, nearly as shocked by the name as by the storm itself. I had dreamed about this storm—it's name, the severity, and now the evasive dream was real. Hurricane Darla was about to hit, and I felt unable to move. The newscast showed video of high winds, heavy rainfall, and flooding. People were advised to find shelter. The entire gulf coast of Florida was an evacuation zone. The hurricane had been heading west, but after slamming down on the west coast of Cuba, it turned north and then northeast, gathering speed, now a category four.

"Wasn't Andrew a four?" "Or was it a five?" "Oh, my God." We were falling over our words as we stared at the blurry screen, mesmerized as the shocking scenes came in and out of focus, with the creeping realization that this was real.

We threw on some old rain capes that were hanging by the door, and then stepped outside into the rain. Darkness was closing in quickly, making it hard to see anything beyond a few feet even with the outdoor lights on. We picked up whatever we could see and lift, tossing things into the shed as fast as we could work. Ben found a two-by-four and shoved it through the handles on the shed door when we were done. The little building sat on a decent foundation, so maybe it would stay put. A huge laurel oak grew next to the trailer, almost leaning on it, its limbs hanging down to offer shade.

As we made our way to the front door, Ben shouted, "That tree might hold the trailer down if we're lucky. Then again, it might come through the roof."

My back felt like it might break as we used our weight to close the door against the wind. The lock barely held as Ben turned the knob, then pulled a chair over to block the door from blowing open. With all the windows closed, and the trailer already smelled musty again. I searched the house for candles and supplies. Like all good Floridians, my brother was pretty well stocked with emergency gear. There was a large flashlight with new batteries next to it, and three unopened gallons of water were lined up under the sink. In his bedroom, I found some large candles in a box that I had sent him. A lighter sat next to his cigarettes on his nightstand, and I had noticed book matches in the kitchen.

We collapsed in front of the television again. I had sent incense along with the candles in my gift box to Larry. I lit several of the sticks to cover up the musty odor. My brother had joked about the incense, asking me if I thought he was planning to entertain some hippies. Thinking about Larry's comment made me smile, and I realized how much I would miss him. I burned incense often; I wondered if he had thought of me as his "hippy sister."

Ben glanced at me and suddenly got to his feet, as if remembering something important. He said he had to make one last trip to his car. It was parked next to the door nearly touching the front of the old Lincoln. The wind caught the screen door, nearly ripping it off its hinges as soon as Ben unhooked it. I leaned against the inside door to keep it shut until he came back in, and we managed to get the chair back in place to hold the door closed.

I was glad I remembered to bring my pain pills and an ice pack, which I removed from the freezer and wrapped in a towel. I sat down with the towel behind my back and picked up my wine glass. My pain was intense. I couldn't believe I lifted such heavy objects off the lawn, surprised at my adrenaline-powered strength. I hadn't done anything strenuous since the accident, careful not to make my injuries worse. *This ought to do it,* I thought. *Then again, whatever doesn't kill me will make me stronger...or so they say.*

"What did you need to get?" I asked. "Insulin, or a gun? I already have one, by the way." Of course I didn't have it with me, but I didn't mention that.

Ben shook out his rain cape and put it over the shower rod next to mine, snickering as he spoke. "I hope you don't mind and I won't smoke if it bothers you, but a friend of mine gave me a bag of pot while I was in New York. I thought it wouldn't hurt to roll a few numbers while we still have some light. It might be a good distraction from the storm. Don't you think?"

I let out a short laugh. "Another lawyer who smokes," I said, thinking about Joe. We both smoked when we were younger, often sharing hits during chess games. The man was ruthless, always won, same as in the courtroom. Diane preferred her cigarettes and refused to play chess with him.

"I guess lawyers only *order* drug tests. Apparently, they don't have to comply themselves. I haven't smoked in years, but what the hell. We probably won't live to see daylight anyway."

"Oh, ye of little faith. Of course we will," he said with profound confidence. "I do think we should try to cover these windows, though. If you'll help me round up some blankets and towels, I'll make use of your brother's toolbox and that jar of nails. Plywood would work better, but I couldn't find any; looks like Larry used up whatever he had when he built that shed."

I forced myself out of the chair and walked around the house, finding a few old blankets and some large bath towels. As I folded the blankets and sized up the towels, Ben hammered them onto the casings, not an easy task because many of the casings were metal and the paneling as brittle as plastic. He somehow managed to attach the coverings, even using duct tape in some areas. He commented that if he had found more tape, he would have used it on the windows to prevent shattering. I remembered doing the same to prepare for Hurricane Andrew.

When the job was done I retrieved my ice pack from the freezer, once again placing it behind my back. While Ben cleaned and rolled his weed, we watched the weather unfold on the screen. Once we decided there was nothing else we could do, I felt a strange calm come over me. I wanted to tell Ben that I named the hurricane long before it had even been deemed a tropical storm, but that could wait until we got good and stoned. I laughed to myself at the thought of getting high at my age, secretly liking the idea and hoping that it would ease my back pain. *Medical marijuana*, I said to myself. Ben looked at me and smiled, as if he'd heard my thought.

All of a sudden there was a loud crash of thunder, and the entire room lit up as though a huge searchlight had turned on us for a split second. As soon as the lightning hit, we lost power. I had placed all the candles together on the kitchen counter. We both jumped up and began lighting candles, as though we were boiling water and ripping sheets to prepare for a home delivery.

After several candles were lined up, we recognized our absurd panic behavior and started laughing. Two strangers, thinking the same way, acting the same way, and he reached out and hugged me at the very moment I was about to hug him. I pulled away quickly, embarrassed by the gesture. I really wanted to be held, but this man was a stranger. It seemed like I'd known him a long time, but the truth was we had met just that morning.

"You're shaking," he said. "Why don't you sit down, and I'll take care of the candles. Okay?"

Things were smashing against the side of the trailer, making me appreciate that the windows were covered, and that we had done all that before the lights went out. Thanks to Ben I felt fairly safe. I had been skeptical at first, about his offer to drive me here and then offering to stay when Larry's car refused to start. Sure he had seemed nice, but nearly everyone seems nice at first. Who could blame me for not wanting to trust anyone? But here we were in the throes of a hurricane, and I certainly couldn't hold any resentment toward this man who was here helping me. I watched as he placed the lit candles around the kitchen and living room, feeling incredibly lucky that he had stayed with me. I prayed silently that we would stay safe, knowing somehow that we would get through this together.

Chapter 6

When Darla Hits

I remembered that I had packed a draft of my book, the first four chapters anyway. I wondered if I should tell Ben about the name. *I still can't believe this,* I thought to myself. *He'll probably think I'm a witch or something; it's pretty weird, even for me.* I'd had other psychic experiences in my life, but had ignored them for the most part. *Maybe I should start paying attention.*

Back when I had finished the first chapter, which at the time was meant to be a short story, I had asked Taylor if he wanted to read something I had written. He hadn't sounded at all enthused when he answered, "Yeah, okay. Maybe later when I get home."

I should have taken the hint, but instead I placed a copy on his nightstand, which he picked up a few days later while I was taking a bath. He was reading the last page when I came back into the bedroom. The television was on and he kept looking up at the screen. He tossed the pages back onto the stand after he finished, and then looked up at me with a patronizing smile.

"Well, do you like it?" I had asked.

"Sure, I guess. The first part's kind of an interesting little scenario. That didn't really happen, did it?"

I swallowed, my throat already tightening up. "Most of it's true; with names changed to protect the innocent," I joked.

"Well, it's a good way to pass the time, I suppose. Have you listed anymore items for sale on eBay?"

"Yes, just as I do every day. The green McCoy vase sold yesterday. You can ship it out as soon as the check arrives."

"How much did we get for it?"

"Thirty-five." I almost hissed the number as I walked out of the room. Tears gathered in the corners of my eyes, and I didn't feel like wasting them on my insensitive husband. He had brushed off the story that I worked so hard on, had felt proud of until now.

Would it kill you to give me a little encouragement? You're always interested in what I sell, how much money comes in. Bastard. My teeth were clenched as the last word came into my head. I wanted to scream it at him but it wasn't in me, nor was it worth the bother. I had grown used to his lack of interest, but I needed some input and hoped he might think my writing was interesting, at least. Instead, he saw it as a good way to pass the time—between listings. I swallowed again. His attitude was often condescending, and when I challenged him about anything, I nearly always lost. Taylor was an excellent debater, and I usually got too mad to think clearly. He hurt my feelings on a daily basis, and whenever he noticed that I was upset, he'd laugh and tell me not to be so sensitive, that he was only joking.

For the last few years I had wanted him to leave, but I knew he wouldn't go even if I asked him to. The mortgage was nine months past due and it would not be paid until or unless I received a settlement or sold the place. We argued about money often since he and Marcel started their business, even more often since the accident cost me my job. My efforts to reason with Taylor were futile. He pointed out that since the mortgage and equity loan amounted to the value of the house, it didn't make sense to try to pay the bank. The way he saw it, if the house was foreclosed on, so be it. My credit rating was no longer viable, anyway. So what if we lost our home? We could always get an apartment until the insurance money came through.

He'll never see a cent of it, I said to myself.

I heard him hang up from a phone call as I was wiping my eyes. He yelled out, "I have to get going. Marcel set up a breakfast meeting with the porn site guys. Shall I bring you something from the diner, Love? A bagel, or a muffin perhaps?"

"No, that's okay. I'll see you later."

As the door swung open, I started to ask him to take the garbage, but stopped myself. I had already asked him twice, and both times he said that he'd do it later. He obviously had much more important things to do. "Shall I bring you a bagel, love?" *What a joke,* I thought, knowing he'd probably have forgotten anyway.

Coming back from my memory, I looked over at Ben as he ran his tongue along the edge of a rolling paper, folding it expertly into the perfect joint. He lit it with a match, took a hit, and then passed it to me. I hesitated, and then did the same. It tasted good, not as much like musty, fertilized earth as I recalled. I coughed lightly as I exhaled.

Without speaking, I picked up a candle and decided to look for a radio. It didn't seem right to get high without music. I made my way down the narrow hallway past the back door. Trying to hold the candle steady so it would stay lit, I stubbed my toe outside my brother's bedroom door. I managed to keep from yelping as I pushed his tackle box out of the way with my other foot. The candle proved to be ineffective, and I was about to go back for the flashlight when I spotted the wrapping paper I had used on Larry's birthday gift, a portable stereo. The box was empty except for the batteries that I had sent along. Figuring the stereo was probably plugged in somewhere, I took the batteries and left the room.

I walked into the bathroom and put the candle and batteries next to the sink, thinking about how nice Ben was to have cleaned the bathroom. As the toilet flushed, I made a mental note not to run to the bathroom too often, so as not to waste the flushes. As I started to open the door, I noticed something long and dark on the shelf by the towels.

With a true Cheshire cat grin on my face, I walked into the living room holding the little stereo. "How would you like some news, and maybe some music?"

Ben said, "Excellent, are there batteries in it?"

As I handed him the package of batteries, he smiled at me and shook his head, clearly pleased with my discovery. He quickly removed the back panel, put the batteries in place, and tuned in a Tampa station that squawked out hurricane warnings from Key West all the way to Orlando. Listeners were instructed to tune in their associate station in Tallahassee if we lost that broadcast. It was probably good that we couldn't see the television coverage; the radio was bad enough.

When Ben noticed my empty water bottle, he asked me if I'd like more water or some wine. I told him that I'd rather have a cup of tea, but since that wasn't possible, another glass of wine would do nicely. I had noticed a second bottle when I emptied the bags, thinking that he had bought one for me and one to bring home with him. I was no longer surprised by his foresight, accepting my good fortune as a gift from the universe.

He touched my shoulder as he handed me the wine. "Don't worry," he said softly. "There's a good stand of trees behind us, and the ocean is a mile away. We have as good a chance as anyone. Better than most, actually."

My brother had used some good foundation materials when he set up his home, and the skirting was firmly attached to the trailer. Larry had been adding on for years, making his mobile home look more like a multi-level barrack. The sheets of corrugated metal roofing overlapped, some areas rusted and worn while other areas appeared to be newer. I remembered him teaching me how to use a hammer when I was seven years old, how I cried when I hit my finger. My big brother held my hand under the water faucet to stop the pain, telling me I wasn't quite ready to be a carpenter. He let me try again a few weeks later, handing me a smaller hammer and reminding me to be careful.

The lights had gone out around midnight, and the next few hours were noisy and scary, the wind so loud it seemed to scream at times. Through it all, we managed to enjoy ourselves. The wine we drank was a Shiraz-Cabernet blend from Australia, blood red with a mild oak flavor and the hint of wild berries. He told me he'd bought that kind before and found it to be quite good. We broke out some cheese and crackers around 4 a.m.

and talked about digging out the charcoal grill from the carport when morning came. We could boil some water for coffee or tea; wishful thinking but it wouldn't hurt to humor each other. The way the wind was tearing around, bending trees and ripping off branches, breakfast seemed like a fantasy. The windows rattled, making the blankets Ben had nailed up, seem worthless. He said he wished he could find some boards, that maybe he should try to get back into the shed.

"Please don't go outside in this, Ben. You could get hurt or blown away, and I'd be left alone. The storm will be over soon, won't it?"

He nodded his head as if to tell me I was probably right, and went about hammering more nails around the edges of the blankets. Then he sat down near the squawking radio, picked it up and tuned in the Tallahassee station. We shared a few hits off a joint, causing my eyelids to grow heavy and I soon fell asleep. I woke suddenly from another crash of some kind. Ben had dozed off on the sofa, with one foot on the floor and his other foot on the coffee table. I adjusted my position and shivered at the sound of the wind thrashing through the trees. My icepack was still cold. I felt grateful for that along with still being alive, saying a silent prayer of thanks. Looking over at Ben, I smiled and dozed off again.

I felt the pain in my leg before I was fully awake. At first I thought I was dreaming when I heard myself moan. By the time I opened my eyes, Ben was lifting me out of the chair. A jagged-edged chunk of terra cotta tile had crashed through the window, hitting my chair and cutting into my leg as it came to rest. The old blanket that Ben had nailed to the window casing was now in shreds, and the wind and rain came whipping through. After Ben placed me safely on the sofa, he hurriedly nailed a throw rug to the window casing in an attempt to secure the window again. I watched the candles flicker as I held onto my leg.

Ben appeared frantic as he took the flashlight into the bathroom, returning with the contents of my brother's medicine cabinet. I lay there confident that he would take good care of me, yet whimpered slightly as he ripped open my pant leg. He poured some hydrogen peroxide on the nasty-looking gash, and then swabbed it with iodine before covering it with gauze and tape. I gasped as the iodine hit my wound.

He whispered, "Sorry...I had to do that. You'll be okay."

As I watched him bandage my leg, I wondered how I would have managed if he wasn't there to help me. The sheets of rain continued, and the wind howling through the trees sounded like a buffalo stampede. I was starting to feel woozy, so I focused on my breathing to prevent the room from spinning. *Breathe; don't get sick...in with the good air, out with the bad air.* I repeated the mantra to myself until the nausea subsided. It felt like a good time to pray again and I did, this time out loud. Ben tightened his hand on mine and said "Amen" with me at the end.

The hurricane center was reporting updates and more warnings for central Florida, Orlando and Jacksonville both in Darla's path as the storm ripped up the gulf coast and tore through the center of the state, still headed northeast, and wide enough to do major damage to half the state. The southeastern coast was being spared except for heavy rainfall and minor wind damage. At least my house would still be standing. Taylor must be pretty anxious; he'd probably be thinking that he shouldn't have let me go, not that he should have come with me. I thought about what a basket case he would have been if he were here, but just as Ben and I made it through the night, Taylor and I probably would have made it too. It just wouldn't have been as easy or as fun, nor would we have done the prep work. I could almost hear Taylor saying that he "wasn't about to go out in the bloody rain and dig for vegetables or scavenge things off the lawn." I was quite sure he wouldn't have bothered to stop for groceries either. I felt a slight sense of pleasure at the thought of him worrying about me. I had called him from the law office and told him that I'd been offered a ride, and that my brother's phone was disconnected.

I smiled as I thought about how much I enjoyed talking with Ben during the night, describing our marriages and sharing our views of the corporate and political scenes. The 2000 presidential campaign was in full swing, the rhetoric obnoxious and tiring. We were trying not to lose faith in our government, agreeing that it hardly mattered who won because the system was so corrupt. I found it hard to believe that Ben was an attorney. He seemed more like a teacher or a carpenter, and I could definitely see him as a doctor. The bandage on my leg had been expertly applied. Talking about politics, relationships, and life in general, helped keep our minds off the storm, and away from the thought that we might not make it out of that trailer, ever.

Ben knelt down to check my bandage. When I looked up at him and smiled, he leaned closer and kissed me, like he had kissed me a thousand times. Nothing passionate or sensual, it was just nice. Even though the kiss surprised me, I didn't turn away. I enjoyed his soft and friendly touch, which somehow felt quite natural at that point. It didn't seem like he had anything improper in mind, and it felt good to be with someone so pleasant and kind, someone who had the common sense to do what needed and glad to do it. He stood up and pulled back a corner of the blanket that was hanging over the side window, exposing a glimmer of light.

The wind had died down slightly, so Ben decided to try opening the back door. Protected somewhat by the shed, it might be a better bet than the front door. A number of things had blown against and around the trailer during the night. I hoped he might salvage the grill as I thought about how much I would love a cup of coffee. I'm sure he dreaded seeing what his beautiful Land Rover looked like. It seemed doubtful that it could have come through the storm unscathed; hopefully he had adequate insurance coverage.

As if he read my mind, he said, "I hope the Rover didn't float away."

"Me, too. It's one of the nicest vehicles I have ever had the pleasure of riding in."

"Glad you like it. I've always wanted one and I found a great deal in New York. It's sort of a celebration gift to myself," he said smiling.

Resting on the pillow that Ben placed under my head, I listened to the wind and rain, now gentle instead of harsh, as I drifted in and out of sleep. Suddenly the door slammed backwards against the wall, jarring me fully awake. Ben stood in the hallway, fidgeting with the latch. The blankets held out most of the light, but a votive candle on the kitchen table glowed enough to show his outline. My heart seemed to beat faster as he came into focus. *Had he really kissed me or had I dreamed that?*

I said, "Are you all right, Ben? How is everything? Your car?"

"It's hard to believe, but except for the fact that we're surrounded by water, we are doing okay. I dragged the grill onto the back porch. It's a good thing we stashed it in the Lincoln or it would be long gone. The canopy that was over the carport blew away. That must have been what we heard last night, when it sounded like the trailer was ripping apart. If all goes well, we'll have caffeine soon."

"Oh, Boy, coffee," I laughed.

He smiled at me and said, "We made it through the night... just like I said we would."

According to the latest hurricane coverage, Darla had weakened to a category three, still moving rapidly through the Sunshine State. Warnings and evacuation routes were still being broadcast, the locations now north of us. We were on the outskirts of Darla's path; much too close for comfort, but feeling blessed that we weren't among the casualties being counted.

Ben had discovered an old coffeepot under the sink while he was looking for duct tape to prepare for the storm. The old aluminum percolator was covered with dust, probably abandoned years ago when Larry bought his first automatic coffeemaker. The *Mr. Coffee* on his counter had also seen better days. Ben washed the coffeepot and filled the basket with coffee grounds. I couldn't help but see him as the perfect man as I watched him go about his chores, which he didn't appear to consider chores. He whistled on and off, as though he were enjoying the whole ordeal. The injury to my leg kept me from helping so I rested and watched, happy that I had thought to bring my pain pills.

Breakfast consisted of grilled biscuits, sliced tomatoes, and boiled eggs. The biscuits I made to have with the pasta had turned out dry and rather bland. Now, toasted on the grill with a little butter, they tasted delicious. The coffee Ben made was excellent; he had added a touch of salt. We talked quietly after we ate, enjoying a smoke with our second cup of coffee.

The sky was dark, and the blankets over the windows made it seem even darker. The storm had passed us, but the aftermath still felt threatening. News reports described flooding and other disasters throughout the southeast. Entire trailer parks were destroyed, along with thousands of acres of orange groves and other produce. Many marinas and beachfront properties were ruined. Twenty-three people were reported dead; more casualties were expected.

We kept the radio at a low volume as we talked, about how his marriage hadn't worked, how none of mine had. I told Ben about how quickly my relationship with Taylor had gone downhill, once we tied the knot. I also told him about my insurance battle, and about the book I was writing.

Ben told me he'd really like to read my book, even though it wasn't finished. He wished he could write anything other than legal briefs; he hated being a lawyer. He had dropped out of medical school after both of his parents died while attending a legal conference in Pennsylvania. They were among several dozen people who contracted Legionnaires Disease. Ben regretted not staying in medical school, instead of transferring to the law school that was his father's alma mater. Overwhelming sadness had clouded his thinking.

He talked about his marriage to Nicole, a spoiled rich girl from Long Island whose father made a fortune in real estate, her mother the classic gold digger. They didn't think Ben was good enough for their daughter, but changed their minds once he graduated from Harvard law school. Nicole wanted Ben to work for her father and take advantage of all that money and corporate acclaim, but he had wanted nothing to do with the family fortune. He realized the marriage was a mistake shortly after the ceremony ended. During the reception, Nicole told him that she didn't want to honeymoon in the country as they had planned, instead accepting an invitation to spend two weeks on a yacht with friends of her parents. The yacht would make an enviable backdrop for all the pictures she wanted to show off to her friends. The newlyweds made love three times in the two weeks, proving to Ben that his bride was more interested in looking romantic than in being romantic.

Ben sounded so melancholy that I decided to tell him about *my* honeymoon, how Taylor had gone fishing every day, after driving into town to buy fish worms or minnows, and a variety of hooks and lures. Not once had he brought me a flower or a gift of any kind; there wasn't a romantic moment during the entire time. He wouldn't even take me to dinner, saying that the only good restaurants were too far away. So I cooked the fish he caught, along with vegetables from a nearby farm stand, lighting candles that he always blew out before we ate. I knew he didn't like to eat out or by candlelight, but this was our honeymoon after all.

My mother-in-law had given me a book by Dr. Wayne Dyer, entitled *How to Have a Happy Marriage* or something like that. In it, the good doctor advised that a new wife shouldn't expect too much from her husband. Just act cheerful and keep praying. Intimacy does not come easily to most men, but it can usually be developed over the years, with chances increasing once he becomes a father. I wondered what had happened to "two people becoming as one." Was that just a line, thought up by some religious zealot to make women want to marry and have babies? And what about brides my age with no children forthcoming?

Ben was in stitches. He thought I was making things up so he would feel better about his own pathetic honeymoon.

"It's not funny, Ben. That's really what happened. And it never got any better. The intimacy never de...de...developed," I said, nearly choking from laughter.

We went from somber to hysterical within a matter of minutes. Once we composed ourselves, Ben got up and went into the kitchen to get me a glass of juice. He mentioned that there was still nearly half a bottle of wine, as well as some sodas and beer that my brother had stashed in the shed.

"There are lots of interesting things in the shed, most of them ruined now. When things dry out a little, I'll fill some garbage bags."

What a mess, almost a blessing that my poor lame brother did not have to deal with this. I missed him, and that feeling gave way to how much I missed my kids. They must be frantic with worry about me, especially Dawn. I wished with all my heart that I could let them know I was fine. Except for the chaos from the storm and the pain I was in, I was having a wonderful time.

On his way back to the living room, Ben noticed that water was creeping in from under the front door. He grabbed some towels to sop up the streams of water that were now running across the kitchen floor, and then wadded up an old blanket and wedged it in front of the door. We hadn't noticed while we were talking and laughing, but the living room rug was already saturated. The incense helped to cover the smell, which was now growing stronger. Soon the water covered all the floors except for my brother's bedroom. That room had been added on and was a step up from the rest of the trailer.

Ben quickly moved what we needed into the bedroom, and now he moved me. I probably could have walked with his help, but he scooped me up off the sofa and carried me. It felt good to be in his arms. As he put me down on the bed, I whispered, "Thanks, Big Guy."

He tucked a pillow under my head and winked. He said, "My pleasure, Sunshine" as he headed for the kitchen to make our lunch. He returned with cheese and lettuce sandwiches and two mugs of beer. It tasted bitter, lukewarm, but I managed to drink part of it while washing down another pain pill.

I was half asleep when Ben covered me with a quilt that I recognized, one made many years ago by Aunt Annie, my mother's oldest sister. Larry had always loved that quilt so Mom gave it to him when he married his first wife. The candle next to the bed cast a soft glow on the quilt, creating a contrast of colors. The pattern was reminiscent of a field, with row upon row of rich, dark earth ready to receive life. Adjacent to this, a quiet pond encircled by cattails, reflected intense sunlight with its vibrant spectrum of brilliant rainbow colors. Meanwhile, imperturbable bovines grazed in a nearby meadow. The perception of weightlessness subdued me as I became removed from reality, the dreamy atmosphere adding to the serenity. The yellow calico sun was at its summit, glaring, unrelenting, without mercy. Soon it would disappear, leaving a mellow darkness as the chill of night steals in.

Falling into a deep sleep, I dreamed about my children when they were small. Dawn was running across the lawn, chasing a butterfly and screaming in delight as she watched the brightly colored insect glide from flower to flower, easily avoiding her touch. Paul Jr. sat on the lawn next to his tricycle staring at the clothesline, where the very same quilt that was now covering me, hung, waving softly in the breeze.

When I woke up, I remembered an essay that my son wrote in the seventh grade, describing his grandmother's quilt. I had been thinking about his words when I fell asleep. His teacher praised his use of vocabulary and gave him an A minus, the best grade he received that year in any subject other than art. He later admitted that another teacher had helped him with the assignment. I had wondered about how he came up with "imperturbable bovines." I missed him so much after he moved away; I missed him still, now more than ever.

As I rolled over, I noticed that the bed was wet. I looked up to see water dripping from the ceiling. Ben was asleep in my brother's recliner and I could hear him snoring softly. He woke up as I was attempting to get off the bed. Rising quickly from the chair, he asked if I was okay and helped me into the bathroom. Then he went back into the bedroom to pull the bed away from the drip, removing the wet bedding and carefully hanging the quilt over the headboard to dry. He piled some of Larry's old work clothes on the floor to catch the drips until he could figure out a way to repair the ceiling.

Standing on one leg, I brushed my teeth and splashed water on my face. My hair felt thick and dirty as I pulled my brush through, and I thought about how nice a bath would feel. The bandage on my leg needed changing, but I would have to let Ben do that. Knowing him, I wouldn't even need to mention it. When I opened the door, I could smell coffee. Ben had put two large candles in a bean crock, and then placed a metal cake rack over the rim to hold the coffeepot. I couldn't believe my eyes or nose, once again in awe of this man. I held my cupped hands against my chin, clapping them like a seal, as I leaned against the kitchen counter anticipating coffee. Ben smiled and shook his head.

The living room carpet was still soggy but the sofa was dry, so I hopped across the wet rug and took off my sandals after I landed on the sofa. Ben handed me a mug of coffee as he sat down beside me. The coffee wasn't nearly as good as the previous morning, but it satisfied my caffeine craving. Ben appeared pleased with himself for thinking of such a clever way to make our favorite brew.

Looking out the window, he mentioned that the water hadn't gone down much, but that it wasn't any higher either. We would have to wait a little longer before we could open the doors, but as soon as the rain stopped again he would open the windows so things could dry out. He spoke about what needed to be done as if they were simple everyday chores, no big deal.

We drank our coffees and talked about getting out of the trailer, and then about getting out of Florida. Ben told me he really missed the country. He had traveled to Vermont a few times, on the ferry that crossed Lake Champlain between Port Kent and Burlington. I remembered many rides on that same ferry, always admiring the views of the mountains around the lake, and the thickly lined trees that cast their reflections in the water. I felt homesick just thinking about it. We talked about riding on the ferry together some day, a silly yet wonderful dream that we could share, at least for a while.

A streak of light shone through the east side of the trailer. Ben pulled off the blanket that covered the window across from the sofa where I sat curled up with my mug of coffee and a fresh number, unlit. According to the latest news, Darla was now crawling through the Carolinas. The storm had lessened further, and was expected to break up at sea. In the meantime thousands of people, ourselves included, were stranded and in need of rescue. Many people had no food or shelter, many of them in danger still. Ben and I felt lucky indeed.

The Tallahassee station wasn't coming in clearly, so Ben tuned in an AM station from Nashville. I wailed along with Janice Joplin singing Bobby McGee, while Ben changed the bandage on my leg.

Afterward, he smiled and said, "There you go, Janice. Are you in pain, or is that just the way you sing?"

We laughed and hugged each other, relieved that the storm was over. I thanked him for taking care of me as he reached for the joint in the ashtray. We sat close together, enjoying our caffeine and smoke, our legal and illicit drugs.

Taylor popped into my mind as I took a hit. What would he say if he saw me now? I knew he and Marcel smoked pot, but I asked them long ago not to bring any drugs into my house. Marcel had nearly died from a heroin overdose, had sworn he would never use again. As far as I knew, he had been true to his word. The two partners often acted like they were still in college together, and it had taken extreme effort to get Taylor to give up some of his old habits. Of course he hadn't given up much of anything, just became more secretive about his activities and the errands he was always running. I felt like a hypocrite, somewhat, but told myself that this was different. Smoking definitely provided a distraction from the storm, *and* it dulled my pain. I felt pretty sure that my smoking days would end once we left the trailer, but now I truly believed that the herb should be legal for medical reasons.

I moved away from Ben and leaned against a pillow on the other end of the sofa. It seemed so odd that I could feel this close to a stranger and so distant from my own husband. I had thought about leaving Taylor for a long time; but the house was mine, and I couldn't sell it and leave the state until my case was settled. If I told him how I felt, he would tell me how foolish I was being and how much he adored me. For years I had pleaded with him to get a normal job and stop treating his partner as if he were our responsibility. They were both incredibly intelligent and capable of making a great deal of money. Even after six years, their business showed little profit, proving that something was seriously lacking in their efforts.

After my accident, I felt that Taylor should step up to bat and take some of my worries away, but he didn't. It seemed more important to him that his business should continue, even though it wasn't supporting us. I sighed and closed my eyes, wondering if things would ever get any better, whether Taylor would ever change.

Ben finished his coffee and stood up. He told me to rest; he would find us something to eat after he washed up.

As I fell into a light sleep, I dreamed about the hurricane, a much milder scene than the real one. In my dream, the trailer floated on the ocean. Boats were bumping into each other, very gently, like they were padded with rubber bumpers. Everything happened in slow motion. I could feel the waves and see the sun breaking through the clouds. I felt happy and I wasn't afraid anymore. Ben was catching fish out the back door, as though the trailer had turned into a houseboat. There wasn't a single problem in the world. I could hear someone on another boat singing an Italian song.

Chapter 7

Bigger Fish

By the time I woke up, Ben had wrung out all of the wet blankets and towels, hanging them to dry in a number of areas. He used a wire previously attached to the carport as a clothesline, now attached to the ski rack on the Land Rover. Several other inventive solutions to unfamiliar problems showed off his Yankee ingenuity and common sense. Raising the furniture up off the wet carpet with blocks of wood and overturned saucepans, and placing the remaining food in the freezer after we lost power, were things I would not have thought to do. I watched as he filled water jugs with the rainwater he collected in pails. There would now be plenty of water for sponge baths, washing dishes, and flushing the toilet. Earlier I apologized for not being able to help.

He scowled and responded, "Aye, you lazy little wench."

The guttural English accent took me by surprise and I burst out laughing. I promised to make it up to him by buying him a wonderful dinner if we ever got out of there.

"I'm afraid it will take more than that," he snapped as he walked out the door.

"Okay, then; a car wash, too," I called after him. I was still half in my dream and wishing it was real.

While Ben worked outside, I managed to climb up on a kitchen stool and check out the top cupboards, finding a number of interesting items. A package of seafood paella that I sent in a gift basket last Christmas, more candles, a Hickory Farms variety box, and a bottle of cheap Scotch. Larry was always a beer drinker—maybe he bought the scotch for company. *Maybe even me,* I thought, wishing again that I had visited him.

Ben came through the door and reprimanded me for being on the stool, frowning and sighing as he helped me down. He seemed pleased with the treasure trove I found, especially the whisky. He maneuvered me to the sofa, ordering me to stay off my leg. Then he took some small glasses from the cupboard and poured us each a drink. He seemed to be having a good time being in charge and finding solutions, taking care of things, including me. As we talked, he told me that he felt like he had known me for a long time, deciding after ten minutes that he would like to know me better. He instructed his secretary to cancel his afternoon appointments while I was on the phone in his office talking to Taylor. I was surprised to hear this, wondering why, and smiling to myself as he continued. He offered me the ride before I made the phone call.

"There's something about you. At first I just wanted to help you because of your brother, then I realized there was a little more to it. You make me feel comfortable; you're down to earth and easy to be with. I enjoy your company."

Looking at him with a silly grin on my face, I raised my hand to hide my smile. I was in my fifties, sporting long brown hair with streaks of gray, a badly damaged back, and now a gimp leg. Looking attractive had never been particularly important to me; I felt much more comfortable looking natural. I had gained nearly twenty pounds since Taylor and I got married, and even though I didn't like my glasses, I hadn't worn my contact lenses since my accident. That accident helped me realize how little either of us cared about each other's looks or feelings.

I sighed as I pulled my mind back to now, slowly raising my eyes to see Ben smiling. A reggae song was playing on the radio, and he was moving his head and one foot to the beat. His smile was contagious, and the music made me wish I could get up and dance.

Ben waited until the song ended, then said, "I wasn't planning to seduce you or anything. I just thought you would be nice to spend time with, and you looked like you could use a friend. Your brother was always talking about how good you were to him. He showed me a picture of you that he took when he worked for your company, on some bridge in Vermont."

That would have been fifteen years ago, before Larry got into trouble again and left the state. He had driven his car off the road and into a brook while he was drinking, then hitchhiked home and reported the car stolen. His keys were still in the ignition, so the police didn't believe his story. He wasn't my best employee, but he *was* my brother. I couldn't remember him taking any pictures, but the bridge I remembered. It was the last job my company was awarded by the state. The contract was completed only weeks before I also left the state. Ironically, neither of us had ever mentioned moving to Florida.

Ben told me what a hard time Larry had after Loretta died. Mr. Minton helped him with some problems during that time. The mobile home was in both their names, but they had never been legally married. I mentioned that I had suspected something like that, because of some differing information Larry offered. Ben commented that maybe I was the one who should be a lawyer.

"A lawyer, no, but maybe a detective; I'm pretty good at figuring things out. For instance, I just figured out that it's about time I learned to use that wheelchair."

The air grew hot and sticky, making me feel listless and weak. My leg hurt worse from my effort to raid the cupboards. I bit my lip to keep from crying out as Ben helped me into the chair. The wheels were hard to turn at first, but with Ben's help I managed to make my way to the bathroom. Once I got through the door, I whimpered as I lifted myself out of the chair and onto the toilet seat. Afterwards I washed my face and told myself to buck up.

By the time I wheeled back into the living room, Ben had put together a rather interesting meal of canned sardines, carrot sticks, and crackers covered with capers and bits of cheese. He arranged the food on my plate to resemble a smiling face. The sardines made a strange smile, carrots flared out to form a nose, with caper eyeballs surrounded by cheese. I couldn't help laughing when he placed my plate on the table.

"You are so silly, Mr. Carmichael. Thank you for that. And for taking such good care of me."

Each time we ate, we treated the food like a gourmet meal, as if it might be our last one. We ate slowly, savoring every bite. We tried to outdo each other with creative menu ideas. Our latest salad dressing, used over carrot strips, onions, and summer squash, was made with olive oil, a touch of wine, and juice from the jar of capers. With a little salt and pepper, it tasted great. There was little food left, so we were making use of every ingredient we could find. We had used up anything perishable, and the canned goods were running low.

As Ben placed the dishes in the sink, we heard the rain start again. He darted outside and gathered all the sheets and towels that were still on the line. The blankets were already dried and folded, stacked on kitchen chairs so they would be handy when we needed them. I looked around at all he had accomplished and wished that I could be more helpful. Coping with back pain during the last two years, I learned how to use my legs to help my back. Now the legs wouldn't cooperate. My left leg throbbed because of a disc pinching a nerve, and now my right leg was injured. There was little room to use my brother's wheel chair, but it kept me off my feet. I watched as Ben took care of everything that needed to be done, feeling waves of gratitude that he was here with me.

Using the same stool that I had foolishly used, Ben found a few more things pushed back on the top shelf. A box of wooden matches, more batteries, popcorn kernels, and a bag of oyster crackers, all covered with a thick layer of dust, were soon placed next to my finds on the counter. He tried to make popcorn but the candle proved to have little effect on the kernels, even though the oil in the pan was bubbling slightly. I suggested that we use the oil to toast the small, stale oyster crackers.

"Brilliant," he said, adding garlic powder and some grated cheese that he found on the door of the refrigerator. He served the crackers with canned green beans, and we sipped scotch with our meal.

I dozed off after I finished eating. When I woke up later, I found myself flat on the sofa. A beach towel was covering me, and two pillows were under my injured leg. Ben was sitting in a chair reading an old *Popular Mechanics* magazine. I hadn't felt him rearrange me; I wondered how long I had slept.

"Are you doing all right?" he asked, as he checked the bandage on my leg. Once again it was spotted with blood, now mixed with oozing green pus. It was obvious that he didn't like what he saw. He had arranged the roll of gauze, adhesive tape, and bottles of iodine and hydrogen peroxide in a small basket, which he referred to as his "med kit." He had been using the roll of gauze sparingly, cutting the strips with small scissors that he sterilized and placed in a sandwich bag. After he cleaned the area and re-taped the bandage, he sat down on the sofa and positioned my feet on his legs. I took a sip of the water he held out, and then fell back to sleep.

The sun was shining through the tiny window in the front door when I opened my eyes. At first I thought I was dreaming, but the pain in my legs and back once again proved I was awake. I looked at my hero who was sleeping sitting up with his feet on the coffee table, my feet still in his hands. When I moved, he awoke and let go of my feet. He stretched his arms out wide, rolled his head back and forth, and yawned. He helped me sit up and offered to get me some aspirin. My stomach was a little queasy, so I passed on the aspirin.

"We'd better lay off the scotch," he said, and I nodded in agreement.

Ben went to work dislodging the grill from underneath the trailer skirt, where it had wedged in the latest winds. He managed to steady the grill's mangled legs with some cement blocks he found behind the shed. Now he needed to find something to start a fire. I vaguely remembered seeing a bright colored bag in the extra room where I came across the flashlight and candles that first night. He went in and rummaged around, finding not only a new bag of charcoal but lighter fluid too. I silently thanked my brother for being so well stocked. Ben used the oven rack to replace the grill rack that was nowhere to be found. He laughed when I clapped my hands in anticipation of coffee.

"The sun is shining, coffee and a hot meal coming up. How lucky are we?"

Ben almost sang the words as he scrambled the last two eggs in a small frying pan, and toasted the last of the bread on the grill. He had filled a saucepan with rainwater, placing it on the grill after our food was cooked. If it boiled long enough, it would be safe to cook the rice. We ate our delicious breakfast and drank our coffee without giving voice to the mess we were in. There was no way of knowing how long we would remain stranded. The floodwater was beginning to creep down toward the road, no longer completely covering the hill we were on but still covering the road with several feet of water.

I took my manuscript out of my briefcase, pulling the title page off so Ben wouldn't see the name until he read it at the end of the fourth chapter. He smiled when I handed it to him, having reminded me several times that he wanted to read it as soon as there was enough light. Even though I had only written a few chapters, it now seemed possible that I might finish it, maybe even get it published someday. That was the first optimistic thought I'd had about my book. Writing helped me stay sane; I hadn't reflected beyond that purpose.

Ben poured hot water into the bathroom sink and placed a fresh washcloth and towel on the vanity. After my sponge bath, which took a good deal of coordination and energy, I wheeled into the smaller bedroom and lay down on the bed. The room smelled of Vicks and was relatively neat, unlike my brother's room. Trudy's bathrobe hung from the door and some stuffed animals sat on her dresser.

I thought about calling my kids. Dawn would surely be going crazy with worry, probably calling PJ and Taylor every few hours, and very likely the Florida state police as well. I had been trying to send them messages telepathically since the storm started. Taylor knew that I'd been offered a ride, so maybe he would try to convince Dawn to stay calm, although that wouldn't do much good. Since my accident, she worried constantly about me. Her anxiety was understandable; I felt the same way when my sister was sick. Taylor got angry each time I flew to Vermont to be with Meg, never sympathetic about why I needed to go so often. I knew my trips strained our relationship, but by that time the marriage already seemed like a lost cause. And my sister was dying; too bad if he didn't like me spending my money on airfare.

I dozed off thinking about how rigid Taylor was. Once he made up his mind, there was no changing it, not that I ever tried real hard. We only went places he wanted us to go. My suggestions to go antiquing or see a movie were nearly always brushed off, causing me to feel rejected and resentful. It pained me to realize that I had reverted to a similar pattern of meekness present in my other marriages. I hoped I would have stood up to Paul if my sister had needed me then, just as I ultimately did with Taylor.

He would be very upset if he knew I had been drinking and smoking, especially with another man, even if the man was just a friend. He didn't like me having fun unless I was with him, and having fun with him had become a rarity. I tried to remember the last time we laughed together. In my dreams I saw Taylor in another woman's arms.

I woke up when Ben walked into the room. He said, "I *cannot* believe that you knew the name of the hurricane! How'd you do that, anyway?"

"Just psychic I guess. I wanted to tell you when they announced it, but I was too shocked to speak. Then I decided that it would be more fun this way."

"That's incredible." He shook his head and took a deep breath. "You've had quite a life, haven't you? I really like your manuscript, and I can't wait to read the book when it's finished."

I smiled and shrugged, not really sure if that would ever happen. But thanks to the hurricane, and Ben, there would be plenty more to write about.

Ben helped me into the wheelchair and pushed me toward the kitchen. As we passed the back door, he said, "The water's been boiling for a while. I guess we can cook the paella now. I'm a little leery about that seafood, but the can isn't swollen, so I guess it's safe. What do you think, shall we give it a try?"

"Yeah, I'm sure it's fine. It isn't that old—only nine or ten months," I said with a shrug. "I'll see if there's an expiration date on the box."

I sat and read the directions as Ben measured out water and opened the can of seafood bits. He hesitated and sniffed the can, then decided to heat the contents separately; we could mix a portion together later since there was no way to refrigerate the leftovers. I placed two teabags in coffee mugs. Ben poured water into the cups and put them on the kitchen table, then pushed my chair closer to the table. The rice was bubbling away, giving off the most sumptuous aromas and making us giddy with anticipation. Even the canned seafood smelled enticing. We had been managing on very little food, stretching everything out, and sharing even the smallest morsels.

"I sure wish we had more of that apple strudel. Maybe we can have a meal at the Alpine Inn when we get out of here," I sighed.

As we waited for the food to cook, we sat at the table sipping our tea and talking. Ben wanted to know more about my family, my childhood, and my marriages. I told him that most of the material in my book was based in reality, almost a memoir in fact; there really wasn't much more to tell. Quickly changing the subject, I asked him to tell me about his own family and childhood.

Hearing him talk about losing his parents, and being an only child, filled my heart with sadness. I had a strong desire to put my arms around him and tell him how sorry I felt that he was alone. Instead I just listened as he talked, allowing my face to register my feelings.

He described a happy childhood, secure and trusting of everyone. His neighborhood sounded more like a fifties television show than a small town in upstate New York. It shocked him to learn that Nicole and her family were so different from the families he knew. I wondered how such a warm, intelligent man could have fallen for such a cold fish. And then I realized how foolish my four marriages must seem to him. We had both hoped to find real love, settling for what we saw as the next best thing, and then trying to make something so wrong, feel right. Obviously, it hadn't worked for either of us.

The paella came out great, both tasty and filling, and there was enough rice for a couple more meals. Knowing there would be food for another day and that there would actually be another day provided an optimistic air. We decided to celebrate with a smoke. We were running low on that too, even though Ben had been smoking very little. He apparently considered the pot to be part of his med kit, being the only thing left that helped my pain. My pain pills were gone, as were my brother's aspirin. I thought about what a nice bedside manner Ben would have if he'd become a doctor, and how much I would miss him once we left the trailer.

Ben heard the motor before I did. As the small boat passed by within view, he pushed open the screen door, waving frantically and yelling as loud as he could. The boat was too far away, and it was doubtful that anyone saw or heard him. We watched together as the boat faded from our sight.

With his arm around my shoulder, Ben said, "Don't you worry, Rosie girl. Another boat will be along."

He gave me a hug as he helped me from the wheelchair onto the sofa. Then he went out to tie my brother's old orange hunting jacket to the antenna on the Land Rover. *Smart*, I thought again.

The trailer had been our home for four days. The hot, muggy weather brought swarms of insects, ranging in size from invisible to humungous. It seemed like there was always something buzzing around our heads or crawling on our skin. My leg seemed to be getting worse even though Ben had been doing everything he could for me. I felt more indebted to him every day. I hoped we would be rescued soon; it was getting harder to deal with the pain, and the pests. Larry's insect repellent had little effect and smelled dreadful, so we stopped using it. I dug out the lavender essential oil that I brought from home, which proved to be much more helpful.

When Ben heard the second boat, I was in the bathroom. He yelled out, "Sweetie, there's another boat."

He called me Sweetie or Sunshine much of the time, affectionate names that made me feel happy. I didn't even mind when he called me Rosie, which was what my brother always called me. I hated the name as a child, but I hated everything about myself back then.

My heart pounded at the thought of being rescued. We could see that the boat was full, but when they were within a hundred yards or so, Ben and the boat's driver were able to communicate by cupping their hands and yelling. Larry's place was not on the rescue list because he was deceased, but they noticed the orange SOS hanging from the Land Rover. We strained to hear as the driver shouted, "Will come back or send another boat, probably not until tomorrow."

"Where do you think they'll take us?" I asked.

"As long as they have a doctor there, it doesn't matter. I'm really worried about your leg. If it isn't taken care of soon... but it will be, and you'll be fine." He touched my cheek and smiled.

I pressed my lips together as tears were welling up in my eyes. The excitement of being rescued, along with the pain and emotions, were too much for me to hide. Ben hugged me and said, "I know."

We celebrated our pending rescue with the leftover rice and a warm beer. Ben placed our dirty dishes in the sink, and picked up empty bottles and cans in an attempt to tidy up. The ashtray held a number of half-smoked joints, which he cleaned and rolled into two new ones. He handed me one to light and placed the other one in the med kit. I felt weak and tired, but I was in too much pain to fall asleep. Ben placed pillows under my legs, trying to make me more comfortable. He put a wet washcloth on my forehead and held my hand as we talked and listened to the radio, waiting for daylight and the sound of another boat.

When morning came, we sipped the last of the bottled water and nibbled on some stale oyster crackers. Ben lit the last joint and made me take a puff every few minutes, carefully stubbing it out each time. The med kit was now empty. He had used the last of the hydrogen peroxide and the final piece of gauze covered my infected bruise. I was growing weaker, but I knew I'd be okay as long as Ben was with me. He rinsed out the washcloth that had been covering my forehead, gently brushing the hair away from my face and dabbing at the insect bites on my neck. He helped me sit up, then put me in the wheelchair and pushed me to the bathroom.

I could no longer get in and out of the chair on my own so he helped me onto the toilet, handing me a towel so I could cover up as I pulled down my pants. I felt embarrassed at first, but too weak to protest. When he came back in the room to help me up, I held onto the towel with one hand and pulled up my sweatpants with the other hand as I leaned on him. He pushed me to the living room and helped me back onto the sofa.

"I'm going to miss you when this is over," he said as he took my hand. "It's been the nicest few days I've ever spent with anyone, even under these circumstances." He put his arm around me and kissed me, very gently. "I sure wish you weren't married."

"Me, too," I said. This time I kissed him back, giving him a hug with all the strength I had left, and then rested my head against his chest.

He sighed and then looked up as we heard the sound of a boat motor in the distance. We couldn't see it, but we could hear it getting closer. Ben placed a clean trash bag over my leg, securing it with a necktie he found in Larry's closet. He said we'd need to keep the wound dry and keep my leg raised.

The boat's engine sounded tired, sputtering and stalling a few times before we got going. We were the only two passengers at first, but the boat soon stopped to pick up a fourteen-year-old boy who was swimming toward us. His parents warned him not to go out, but the storm had passed and he convinced them that he'd be safe. His small rowboat capsized when he tried to pull a piece of driftwood from the water, just minutes before our boat came along.

By the time we reached the small clinic, all of us were soaked by the rain that had started once again. Ben held me close to him throughout the ride, making sure that my leg was covered and keeping me warm. He and two aides helped me into a wheel chair once the boat was safely docked. Inside the clinic, he pushed me to a pay phone so I could call my family.

He didn't listen to the call, probably assuming that I would call Taylor. Instead, he went to the men's room and washed up, and then spoke to the nurse who was manning the front desk. She handed him a form to fill out.

Dawn broke down in tears when she heard my voice. "Oh, Mom. I was so worried about you; I've hardly slept since I heard about the hurricane. I must have called Taylor a hundred times to see if he'd heard from you."

We talked through our tears for a few minutes as I described my injury. I gave her the number at the clinic and told her I would call her back the next day. She said she'd call her brother and let him know I was safe, and she asked me if I wanted her to call Taylor.

"No, Honey, I'd better call him. You call PJ and Carrie. Oh, and Aunt Claire, Okay? She's probably worried too."

Taylor sounded relieved when he heard my voice, not frantic by any means. I told him that I was okay except for my leg, but that I had to stay put until help arrived. I didn't mention Ben; I could tell him about my adventures when I got home. He didn't offer to come and get me, but I knew he wouldn't have made it anyway. Everything west of the everglades was still flooded, and besides, I would need to be hospitalized until my leg was better. He asked how I hurt my leg and I told him what had happened. His voice changed from feigned concern to pronounced agitation.

"Damn it, Rose, I knew I shouldn't have let you go. I don't know why you always end up being the one to take care of all the family affairs, especially since you have so many brothers and sisters."

"Taylor, I have to go. They need to admit me and check out my leg. And as for all my brothers and sisters, there aren't as many as there used to be."

I hung up before he could apologize, if in fact that was what he had intended to do. I took a deep breath, then looked down at the blood on my sweatpants. Taylor's face left my mind as soon as Ben was next to me again. The admitting process was somewhat disorganized, but I was eventually placed in a nice, dry bed. I thought that I should tell Ben he could leave, but I didn't want him to go. After I was settled in my hospital bed, he went to make some calls.

The clinic was in a town called LaBelle; neither of us had ever heard of it. I noticed three other cots in the room, each holding a sleeping body and separated by a hanging curtain. I thought I could smell ammonia or sulfur. A cart rattled down a nearby hallway and the room seemed to swirl as the pain medication kicked in, sending me into a deep, delicious sleep.

When I woke up, Ben was sitting in a chair next to my bed. His eyes were closed. Bright blue numbers on the clock read 10:30. *Probably p.m.*, I thought, not only because of the darkness but because I felt too tired to have slept through an entire night.

Ben opened his eyes and asked quietly, "How are you doing?"

"I'm fine," I whispered, "a little groggy but thankful for the medication. I'm so glad you're still here."

He smiled. "I found a place to spend the night, but I didn't want to leave until you woke up."

"Where will you be staying? Will you be coming back here?"

With a sigh, he smiled and nodded his head. "Of course, silly woman; I'll be here as long as you are. The motel's just down the street, and the number is right here by your bed if you need me. I'll be back in the morning. Is there anything you want me to bring you?"

"Yeah, coffee."

He laughed softly as he pushed my hair from my face, then bent down and kissed me on the cheek. "Okay, Sweetie. I'll see you in the morning. Have a good sleep."

After he left, I thought about the events of the week. I had traveled to my brother's expecting only hassles. Now I was at the end of an adventure, a rather romantic adventure at that. This wonderful man had stayed with me and cared for me through a hurricane. He never once got upset or angry, not even when his brand new vehicle got trashed. I couldn't think of anyone who had ever been as generous or as kind to me, and he cared enough not to leave me here alone. As I drifted off to sleep, I knew that my new hero would star in my dreams.

Chapter 8

Another Day In Paradise

I heard voices outside my room, but I couldn't make out what they were saying. The door opened, and Ben stepped in carrying a huge bouquet of roses, bright yellow ones. "For all the sunshine you have brought to my life," the card read. I laughed and hugged him. The nurse who was recording my stats looked up and asked where he managed to find flowers like that in this area? Earlier she had called it a one-horse town, anxious to return to her regular duties in Tampa.

"There's a florist truck parked in front of the clinic. They have extra flowers."

"Thank you, Ben," I said as I pulled one of the open blooms from the milk glass vase.

As I held it to my nose, its scent filled my nostrils and lifted my heart. Yet in the next moment, I felt a wave of sadness. Soon Ben would be returning to work, I supposed. Today was Thursday; the doctor said that I would need to stay for a week to ten days. He couldn't possibly stay here that long.

To my surprise Ben arrived every afternoon and stayed late each night. When I asked him why he hadn't gone home, he asked if I was getting sick of him. "Never," I replied. We'd both have to go home soon, but we chose not to think about it. We talked about other things, never lacking in subject matter, often reflecting on the storm and laughing about our exotic meals.

By Saturday the roads were passable, so Ben hitched a ride back to Larry's place to get his Land Rover. He said it still ran great in its filthy, dented condition. And considering what others had lost, he couldn't feel bad about a damaged vehicle. He brought me a special gift from the trailer, Aunt Annie's quilt. He dropped it off at the dry-cleaners on Saturday, and didn't mention it during his Sunday visit. On Monday afternoon, he came in and placed the quilt on the foot of my bed, a huge smile on his face. He asked if I would let him bring me home when I was released from the clinic. We would get to spend a few more hours together that way. I was touched by the gestures, both the quilt and his offer to drive me home.

After giving the idea some thought, I said, "Well, I don't know how Taylor will like that, but you've been my guardian angel and I'm pretty sure you saved my life. That will have to do. It isn't at all necessary, though, so it's okay if you change your mind." In my heart, I hoped that he wouldn't.

He went on about which route I might enjoy most, and then informed me that he considered buying my brother's property.

"I can sell the trailer, then build a nice house on the land, maybe a cape, with a good storm shelter. You can bet we'll be ready for the next hurricane."

Another nurse came in to change my bandage and check my blood pressure, so Ben left to buy us dinner. I wondered if he was serious about buying the property, or if he was just trying to amuse me. It seemed like an eccentric idea, but then people have done stranger things. I smiled as I remembered him saying, "We'll be ready."

My leg was healing, but it had been badly infected. The doctor told me that if Ben had not taken such good care of me, the infection would have gotten much worse. "You could have lost your leg," she added with a look of concern.

Ben did an excellent job as caregiver. When I thanked him for that and for still being there, he said, "No problem. You'd do the same for me, wouldn't you?"

I felt quite sure that I would do anything for him, nodding my head in response to his question.

Taylor never called once while I was there. When I mentioned that I should probably call home, Ben dialed my number and handed me the phone, then left the room while I talked to Taylor. My arms were sore from all of the needles and IV's stuck in me, so I placed the phone on my pillow and talked. The call didn't last long. I reported my condition and asked about the pets and finances. Taylor didn't say much, just asked when I'd be home. A few times I thought he might be hiding something, or maybe I was just transferring my own secrets onto him. I wondered if he could tell, or if he cared.

When Ben left that night, I missed him desperately. I realized that I hardly thought about Taylor anymore, that I hadn't missed him the entire time I'd been gone. It bothered me that I couldn't remember having ever really loved him; surely I loved him at one time. The doubts kept me awake most of the night, tossing and turning, wishing my life wasn't so complicated. I called home again the next morning, hoping that his voice would make me remember loving him.

He sounded sleepy, and not at all happy to hear from me. "Why are you calling so early? I didn't get to sleep until three o'clock. When are you coming home, anyway?"

"I can't walk yet. And if you're so concerned, why haven't you come to the clinic, or at least called?"

He told me he was sorry, that he had a lot going on and that someone needed to be there to take care of things. I could tell that he resented my being away, even if I was in a hospital. It didn't seem like he missed me, only that he disliked the responsibilities of taking care of the house and the pets. Neither of us bothered to say, "I love you," when we hung up.

Ben came in carrying a box of hot biscuits and two large coffees. He could tell I'd been crying. "What's wrong, Sweetie?" he asked as he put the box down.

I told him about the phone conversation and about how badly I had missed him.

"Why don't you just stay here? Let me call Taylor and tell him that I'm representing you."

I sighed. The thought was very appealing. Taylor wasn't a good husband or even a good companion, but I was still his wife and it was up to me to change that. This wasn't something I could do over the phone; it would need to be done in person.

On Tuesday I called Dawn to discuss my plans. "I've decided to come up and stay with you after my insurance claim is settled. Check around for a good orthopedic surgeon, will you? I still need surgery on my back. My leg is healing pretty well, so I'll probably be released from here within a few days. Then it's back to good ole fart Lauderdale, for the time being, anyway."

She laughed and said, "I will absolutely find you a great doctor, Mom. Kate and I miss you so much and we want you here. Have you told Taylor yet?"

"No," I said. "I want to talk with my lawyer first, and I haven't figured out what to do about the house. But I can't stay in Florida much longer; I'll go crazy if I do."

As I hung up I realized how much I would miss Ben, dreaming that somehow he could be included in my future. I knew that was too much to wish for; I was being foolish to think it could happen.

That evening Ben and I sat next to each other as we listened to an old Phil Collins song, *Another Day in Paradise*—one of the ten-in-a-row oldies but goodies being played on the Tuesday night "Good Riddance to Darla" special. We both had tears in our eyes as we held hands and listened to the song. Earlier I told him that I didn't think he should drive me home.

"I don't want to try to be a good actress, it just wouldn't work for me. Taylor would see the look in your eyes when you look at me, and I don't know what my look might say. I'm afraid it would be obvious that we're more than friends. I don't love Taylor, but I'm married to him, and until that changes…" I shook my head.

By the time the song was over, we had wiped our eyes and managed a smile. I wondered if when this week was over, would we be over, too? Darla brought us together, and now life would almost certainly tear us apart. Regardless of how close we had become, I didn't dare ask for more than friendship with Ben, at least until my life got straightened out. Maybe our feelings weren't as strong as they seemed. Only time would tell.

By Wednesday I felt almost like myself, having taken a shower and washed my own hair for the first time since I arrived at the clinic. As I put on the dark green chenille robe that Ben bought for me at the K-Mart in Fort Myers, I hugged myself and pretended his arms were around me. Knowing that hospital gowns were in short supply at the clinic, he also bought me some nightgowns and a pair of pajamas. Still sleeping at a nearby motel, he drove to his office early each morning and returned to the clinic in the afternoon, an hour's drive each way. The thought of his arrival filled my days with anticipation and happiness.

I waited until lunchtime before calling Taylor to tell him that I might be home by the weekend. He asked whether he would have to come and get me.

After a brief pause, I answered slowly. "I suppose I could take a taxi to Orlando and fly home from there." I hadn't intended to suggest that, but it sounded like an excellent idea as I heard the words tumble from my mouth.

"That'll work. Saturday's better for me. I have tickets to the Dolphins game Sunday. So let me know for sure."

I felt guilty about spending time with Ben, until the game comment. My husband wasn't even planning to stay home and take care of me. The sad part was that it didn't surprise me. I said, "Okay, I'll call you when I know then," and hung up the phone.

When Ben came in, I was brushing my hair. "Wow, you look nice. Are you wearing makeup?" He leaned down to take a closer look.

It was the first time I had applied any form of makeup to my face since we met. A volunteer offered me some Avon samples and I accepted. I didn't usually wear makeup, except for mascara now and then. It felt good to know I could still put on a pretty face if I wanted to.

I smiled up at him. "I'm feeling much better today. The doctor may release me early."

The smile on his face faded, and he looked at me through squinted eyes as if he were in pain.

"Don't be sad, I have a surprise for you. I've decided to fly home from Orlando on Saturday. Until then, I'd like to stay in a nice place and rest for a few days. Would you care to join me?"

Ben didn't have time to respond before the door opened, but his smile was back and I took that to be his answer. My doctor came in, and she agreed that I could leave. Beds were needed for other survivors who were being brought in. She instructed me to stay off my feet as much as possible and to get plenty of rest. I thanked her and assured her that I would do exactly that.

We gathered my belongings and I signed the release papers. The nurses told Ben to take good care of me. I smiled and said, "He always does," and we thanked them for being so nice. Once outside, Ben helped me from the wheelchair up onto the front seat of the Land Rover. It had been washed and dried out, smelling almost new again. Everything else was cosmetic and could wait. He didn't seem at all concerned, said that he'd have it fixed when he got around to it. I knew he meant after he had nothing better to do, after I was gone.

It felt wonderful to be out of bed and back in the world, a light wind blowing and the sunshine warm on my skin. Work crews were cleaning up debris along the roadside, filling dump trucks with destroyed building materials and mangled objects.

Ben stopped at a store before we headed north on Route 29. This time he came out with a small bag of snacks and drinks for the ride. The radio was tuned to a soft jazz station, pleasant to listen to so I didn't bother to check out his CD case. He placed the bag between our seats and leaned over to give me a hug. I kissed his cheek and took a long smell of his aftershave as I hugged him back. The light scent of mint lingered as he slowly pulled away.

He winked at me and said, "Shall we try this again, Sunshine?"

I nodded my head and smiled. "Let's do. This will be the last time I'll get to be waited on, so I might as well take advantage of it," I joked. I took a deep breath. "And we'll have to maintain our platonic status. I can't be intimate with you, not yet anyway. I hope that's okay with you."

"Yet," he said and smiled. "I can handle 'yet.' That means there's hope for someday. There's a reason we're together, even if it's just to learn from each other. Whatever happens, I'm happy to share any relationship you can live with. I'm not interested in a fling any more than you are."

As I listened to the music, I remembered Ben telling me that he had never been happy in his marriage, even though he tried hard to make it work. His wife came from a high-society family on Long Island and he came from a rural area in upstate New York. The difference was drastic, like being from another country, not just another county in the same state. There were problems from the moment they became engaged, even though Nicole had insisted on the engagement. She and her mother shopped for the ring, paying far more for it than they admitted to Ben.

I came back to reality when Ben spoke. "You're being awfully quiet. Are you thinking about Taylor?"

"Actually, I was thinking about you and Nicole."

"I filed the divorce papers before I went to New York—five months and it's final. I was planning to tell you that. I just haven't thought much about her lately. If you have any questions, though, I'm happy to answer them."

"No, no questions. I was just thinking about some things you told me. I'm glad you're not with her anymore. She doesn't deserve you." I noticed he no longer wore the ring.

We decided to stop for coffee on Route 27. A homemade sign advertising a HURRYCANE SALE was propped up against boxes of damaged goods in front of the store. Inside, the place smelled rancid. I was glad I didn't need to use the bathroom; maybe there would be a nice, clean gas station on Route 4. Neither of us drank the coffee we bought, suspecting that the store's water might not have been bottled. We stopped for gas further north, buying more coffee there after we used the facilities. I felt drowsy, glad to have some caffeine to perk me up. I took a pain pill with my coffee.

As we drove away, Ben said, "We'll be in our nice comfy room within the hour. I'm so glad we can stay together for a little while longer. I'll take good care of you. Thank you for letting me."

With a laugh, I said, "You are very welcome."

A convoy of army trucks passed as we pulled out of the gas station, miles of camouflaged vehicles. The sight brought tears to my eyes; so many people needed so many things, and tons of supplies were headed their way. Donated items had been dropped off at the clinic while I was there, and volunteers appeared regularly. I didn't try to hide my emotions as tears streamed down my face. Ben reached over and took my hand, and we rode the rest of the way in silence. The sun was starting to set as we reached the hotel.

Our incredible room offered every amenity one could ask for. The walls held original art, and the linens were far nicer than the standard hotel issue. As I admired the décor, Ben started preparing for my comfort. He fluffed the pillows on my bed and placed my toiletries on the vanity. Although I'd been dreaming about taking a bath since we were in the trailer, I hadn't mentioned it. Yet here he was already filling the tub.

I called out, "Will you be attending to my massage as well, sir?"

As he came out of the bathroom, he looked at me with wide-open eyes and said, "Umm, you'd better watch out, young lady. You could get yourself in a heap of trouble. I suppose I could rub your back later, if you like."

I snickered as I left the room. "Young lady? Hah."

After I closed the bathroom door, I removed my clothes and stepped into the aromatic, steaming bath. Ben had added some of the complimentary bubble bath and a few drops of my lavender oil to the water. I heard his voice on the phone ordering room service, and then the sound of classical music. "How lovely is this?" I thought to myself as I slipped fully into the spacious marble tub. My wound was covered with a clear, waterproof bandage. The stitches formed an interesting design on my leg, reminding me of a lightning bolt that I'd seen on one of my son's record covers when he was a teenager. I tried to remember the band, maybe Judas Priest, no, AC/DC.

Ben knocked lightly on the bathroom door before he pushed it open. Surrounded by bubbles, my breasts were partially exposed as I reached to take the glass of wine, using my other arm to cover up. He noticed my modesty and told me to take my time as he left the room smiling. The warm bath and cool wine brought the perfect ending to a perfect day. We had seen a spectacular sunset as we reached the hotel. It seemed later than eight o'clock; I could easily fall asleep, especially if I got that back rub.

Imagining Ben's touch made my body tingle and I felt a surge of energy. I climbed out of the tub and slathered lotion on my damp skin before wrapping myself in the luxurious robe that hung on the door. The plush terry cloth had a soft, velvety weave, the color of lemon sherbet. This was the most tasteful hotel room I had ever stayed in, far nicer than the flashy casino suites in Atlantic City, one of the places Glen liked to gamble. None of those rooms had the plush, spa-like feeling that this one evoked.

Dinner was delicious: Cornish hens with wild rice and steamed vegetables, served with salad and fresh sourdough rolls. Ben traded his rice for my roll after noticing that the rice was loaded with blanched almonds, something he didn't care for. He had ordered a pot of chamomile tea to help me sleep, and we drank some with our desert—slivers of cheesecake dribbled with a dark chocolate sauce. The china teacups had a delicate violet pattern, and the surface felt silky to my touch, using one hand as a saucer each time I took a sip.

After he placed the serving tray outside our door, Ben helped me get comfortable on my bed and then brought me a second cup of tea. He had requested two queen-sized beds instead of one king size, making me feel completely at ease. We planned to watch a movie, but my eyes grew heavier with each breath. I placed the teacup on my nightstand and didn't wake up until morning. I slept in my robe, and Ben covered me with the comforter from his bed to avoid waking me.

I was sitting in a chair reading the menu when he woke up. He looked at me and smiled. "Well, good morning. Just to let you know; you missed a really good movie, and I was forced to drink the rest of that wine all by myself."

"That wine was excellent, very smooth; German wasn't it? I don't usually go for Rieslings but that one was nice, not too sweet. Sorry I fell asleep on you, but it's nice to have a clear head on my first day away from the clinic. I'm a little achy, though, so I could still use that back rub."

He laughed softly and ruffled my hair as he slowly swaggered past me into the bathroom wearing gray silk boxers. Nice, I thought to myself as I picked up the phone and dialed room service. We ate on our balcony as we read the local paper and enjoyed our first morning together in a real paradise. I felt so happy to be here, and I commended Ben for finding the perfect place for us to relax.

Florida really was a nice place to visit even if it wasn't where I wanted to live. The palm trees were alive with birds that seemed to perform just for us. Small green parrots and bright red cardinals competed for our attention, along with the mockingbirds that chased and mimicked the other birds. The birds seemed as happy as we were that the hurricane had passed, and that the world was beautiful once again.

We spent the next two days relaxing under the palm trees or sitting on our balcony, which overlooked a large man-made lake. The area reminded me of the Grand Bahamas; even though we were next to a lake instead of the ocean, it had a similar feel. I flew to the Bahamas to visit Colleen while she was on vacation a few years back. I had a fabulous time there, eating fresh fish and exotic fruit from the buffet table, and sitting in the cabana sharing pitchers of Sangria with my friend. Colleen insisted that I join her, despite Taylor's protests, even offering to pay my airfare so he wouldn't try to keep me from going. She gave me a hard time for having to ask his permission, becoming almost as annoyed with me as I was with myself. My passive behavior was pathetic, allowing my husband to use my frequent travel to Vermont to guilt me out of doing anything just for fun.

My feelings of resentment disappeared as Ben suggested that we go there together someday. "I'd love to meet your friends," he said. "My best friends live in Manhattan. James works as a stock analyst and his wife Laurie's a pediatric nurse."

"I met Collie in accounting class at a community college in Vermont. We both hated the class, and accounting. One night we decided that we'd rather count margaritas than digits. We've been tight ever since. She'd like you."

On Friday we browsed through a bookstore and a small boutique, both located just off the lobby in the hotel. Ben helped me choose a soft orange jersey and a colorful sarong skirt to wear to dinner. He persuaded me to try on some comfortable-looking Italian leather sandals, and then insisted on buying them for me. I felt like a schoolgirl or a new bride, allowing myself to enjoy every minute of it.

When I thought about Taylor, I imagined myself on a distant island or in another country, instead of only half a state away. I wasn't concerned about adultery; Ben and I had already settled that. I may have been falling in love with this man, but I wasn't being unfaithful, at least not in the Biblical sense. My conscience was clear, accepting my choice to spend time with Ben and entertaining the possibility that my life might be happy someday. And if this was to be the only cheerful time I would get to enjoy, then I was determined to make the most of it.

I had called Taylor earlier in the day to let him know what time to expect me on Saturday night. He suggested I call him before getting on the plane so he wouldn't forget to pick me up. "Write it down, Taylor. And be there," I sighed. He laughed and responded, "I was only kidding, for crying out loud. You have absolutely no sense of humor."

That night Ben and I dined in the hotel restaurant and we planned our final day together. Check out time was at noon, so we decided to spend the afternoon in a park near the hotel. We had driven by one with a large aviary, duck ponds, and lavish flower gardens. We would buy some food for a picnic and enjoy our last day in paradise. Then I would buy him that dinner I had promised him. And then I would fly away home.

Ben and I had just finished our dinner when we heard the band start playing in the adjacent room. He asked me how my leg was doing.

"I think I might be able to handle a slow one," I answered smiling.

After he signed the check, Ben held my chair and helped me up by my elbow. We walked into the lounge, and he pulled me close to him before we were even on the dance floor. The band was playing an old Fleetwood Mac song, *Gold Dust Woman.* We didn't really dance, just held each other and swayed slowly to the music. When the song ended, we took a corner table and listened to the rest of the set. The music was wonderful but a little too loud; it had been ages since either of us heard a live band. When they took a break, we walked to the elevator with our arms around each other's waist.

When we got back to our room, I felt a little worried about my vow to stay chaste—platonic already didn't apply. Ben sat me down on one of the chairs. He pulled the other chair close so that our knees were touching, then he took my hands in his. I felt grateful that he chose to sit on chairs instead of one of the beds. We sat for several minutes, just looking into each other's eyes before he spoke.

"This is hard, Sweetie. I meant what I said about not needing to be with you intimately, but let me know if you feel differently. The longer we're together, the more I want to make love to you. I'll miss you so much when you leave."

I brought his hands to my lips, hugging them and rubbing them against my cheeks, wishing with all my heart that we could be together. His knuckles were wet from my tears when I finally answered.

"Believe me, Ben, I feel the same way. But I don't want to bring anything bad to something that feels so good. Guilt and shame could do that. Let's not chance it; let's do things right."

He closed his eyes and said in his softest voice, "Okay, Sweetie. I can wait."

Eventually we settled in for another evening of being old married folks, without the sex. Steve Martin's movie, *The Jerk*, was on television, and we decided to watch it. Neither of us laughed much; the antics that would normally have me in stitches seemed foolish and clumsy. We sat on the same bed with big fluffy pillows behind our backs, shoulder to shoulder, holding hands. By the time we fell asleep, my head was on his shoulder and his arms surrounded me. When we woke up in the middle of the night, he kissed my temple and whispered "hello" in my ear. We fell asleep with the television on, waking up to a documentary about international waterways, and how much pollution was being dumped into them. Dead fish floated in a body of water as Ben switched it off.

We fell asleep again in a similar position, his arm over mine, holding both of my hands in his. He kissed my neck when he awakened, and hugged me tight before reaching for the phone to order coffee and bagels.

After we ate, I took another scented bath. When I emerged from the bathroom, the drapes were closed and Ben had lit some candles. He motioned for me to lie down, then massaged my shoulders and back with a gentle firmness that stretched my muscles without hurting my damaged spine. He had purchased a book called Healing Therapy and some massage oil, while I was trying on clothes at the boutique. His touch was gentle but firm, and totally relaxing. Mesmerized by the smell of the oil, a blend of bergamot and rosewood, I wished the morning would never end. My nirvana was interrupted as the phone rang, alerting us that checkout time was near.

Pulling my robe closed as I rolled over, I said, "Thank you, Ben. That was absolutely wonderful. You may have found a new vocation."

Ben whispered, "You're welcome, Sunshine." His kiss was soft and sweet, almost innocent. He didn't take any other liberties, just gave me a final hug and then stood up. Had he given me a massage the night before, I doubted we would have stayed strong.

I dressed in the bathroom while Ben gathered our things, carefully wrapping the candles and oils for me to take home. Tears ran down my cheeks as I brushed my hair. I wanted to return to that bed and make love to Ben. Instead, I dried my eyes and finished dressing. If this was the love I had dreamed about my whole life, and I felt certain that it was, then that part could wait.

Chapter 9

Saying Goodbye

"What a beautiful day for a picnic," the clerk commented as we placed our purchases on the counter. Crackers, cheese, hummus, fruit, and Perrier, along with two non-breakable wineglasses were placed in the bag. Ben smiled at her and said, "Thank you," as he picked up the bag and followed me out the door.

The hurricane did a good deal of damage to the park, but the area had been thoroughly cleaned and repairs were in progress. We drank the sparkling water like wine. I wondered what others thought of us as we held hands and watched the birds, the work crews, and the other visitors. Would they have guessed we felt so desperate?

The afternoon was filled more with silence than with laughter and conversation. We found solace in each other, in our unspoken love. Ben leaned against a tree as I rested my head on his chest. His chin touched my head as he played with my hair and rubbed my neck and shoulder, giving me a gentle squeeze whenever his hand reached my arm. I felt so right being with him, often turning to give him a hug and touch his face. His hazel eyes seemed greener today, often dampened with tears just as mine were. Eventually we picked up the remains of our picnic and the large beach towel that we'd been sitting on, heavy sighs and melancholy glances our main form of communication.

My flight to Fort Lauderdale was scheduled to leave at 9:12 p.m. As much as I disliked living in Florida, I especially disliked the Lauderdale area. To me, the place had a weird detached feel about it, as though the residents were escapees, either from distant cities or nearby islands. Dade County, further south, seemed even worse than Broward. I had never felt at home in south Florida, and now felt only apprehension about returning. How I dreaded getting on that plane, and then getting off.

The concierge had raved to Ben about a fabulous restaurant, located close to the airport. We couldn't have found one with better food or a more romantic atmosphere. Each table displayed fresh flowers, crisp linens, and small art deco style lamps that cast a warm glow through frosted mica shades. The scallops I ordered were fresh and plump, with just the right touch of garlic and ginger. Ben's salmon tasted equally delicious.

During our ride to the restaurant we had tried to entice each other by talking about our favorite foods, in a feeble attempt to keep our minds off saying goodbye. Once the food was in front of us I didn't feel all that hungry, but the delightful aromas and splendid presentation quickly drew out my appetite.

We stretched the meal out as long as we could, picking at each other's plates as though we were trying to share more than the food. We had shared everything for over two weeks, falling in love in the process, now feeling that we belonged together. Everyone at the clinic and the hotel had treated us like a married couple, and it almost seemed real...until today. How I wished the fantasy could continue. As we sipped our wine and ate our food, we could no longer hide our sadness or our hopelessness, and we stopped trying to pretend. We looked at each other with longing eyes and brave faces, not wanting to make it any harder yet unable to dismiss the heaviness we both felt. It didn't seem fair that our time together was coming to an end; we had just begun.

Standing next to the Rover, we held each other and promised to talk soon, try to work things out so that we could be together. Boarding time neared as we walked slowly into the airport holding hands. Ben clung to me as we listened to the flight announcements. He asked me once again if I could change my mind, stay just one more day. I knew another day would not make leaving any easier. Tears were already dropping from my eyes.

"Ben, I can't. This is too hard; I don't want to say goodbye again. I'll call you tomorrow, and I'll come back to the trailer in a few weeks. I still need to take care of my brother's estate. ...I can't wait to see you again. In the meantime, though, I need to talk with Taylor about my unhappiness. I decided to leave him long before I met you. Now I'm *sure* it's over, but he's still my husband and it takes time to untangle a mess like this." I wrapped my arms tightly around his neck and whispered, "Thank you for all you've done for me. You know I love you."

"I love *you*, so very much..." he sighed. "Call me the first chance you get."

He kissed me again and squeezed my shoulders as I started to pull away. I missed him already and could feel more tears building in my eyes. I would be home in less than an hour, but I could hardly think of it as home. As I took my seat on the plane, I thought about when I'd be able to see Ben again. My birthday was in two months. I didn't want to wait that long, but it certainly would be nice to spend my birthday with him—what an incredible gift that would be.

Taylor rarely did anything special for my birthday. On my fiftieth, he hadn't even wished me a happy birthday. I waited all day, and nothing. When I confronted him about it, he told me he didn't think I'd want to be reminded that I was fifty. It was obvious that he was the one who didn't want to be reminded; he wasn't even forty yet. I spent the evening alone in my room, upset for days, and too hurt to tell anyone about his comment. He apologized eventually, explaining that choosing gifts was not his forte.

I shook off my resentment by thinking about Ben. He was the most amazing man I had ever met, and he loved me. Whatever he saw in me that caused him to feel that way, I felt grateful to possess. We had grown completely comfortable with each other, no pretensions or mistrust. Being together seemed like kismet, and even though the timing was bad, the feelings were real. I was sure of that, more sure than I had ever felt about anything.

When the flight attendant announced that the plane was nearing the airport, I slipped back into the sad reality that I was about to land in Fort Lauderdale. It would probably be hot and humid outside, as always, so I took my sweater off and put it in my bag. I reached up for my briefcase in the overhead compartment as the line started to move forward, feeling a sharp pain in my leg as I stretched. I had barely lifted a finger since leaving the clinic and didn't realize that my leg was still quite sore.

Taylor stood waiting for me at the gate. He hugged me and gave me a quick kiss when I reached him.

"Hi, Taylor. You have a new shirt. Did your mother buy it for you?"

"No, I bought it. Had some time to kill one day, so I bought a few things. You're always telling me to buy some clothes."

"It's nice. I like the color—blue looks good on you. I bought a few things, too."

He took my bag and we made our way to the car, my old Buick, our only vehicle now. The car survived the accident just as I had, but it had been repaired; so far, I hadn't. I would buy myself a new car, something safe, as soon as my insurance settlement arrived—positive thinking. I resented the fact that every time I needed to use the car, I had to arrange it with Taylor, work around his schedule. After his latest vehicle broke down, he never bothered to buy another one, insisting that we'd save on insurance and maintenance. He didn't see why I needed a car when I wasn't working outside the house. I found it inconvenient as hell, and not at all fair. Not that I drove much anymore, but still.

I thought that Taylor would pepper me with questions, how I was rescued, whether I was scared. But he didn't. He didn't seem to notice that I had lost weight or that I was limping, either. He had never been fond of talking while he drove, so I didn't find it all that strange that he stayed silent most of the way; we could always talk when we reached home. I sat quietly and stared out the window at the same endless city that is always the view in south Florida.

The house was relatively neat. Taylor had obviously made fast work of putting away strewn laundry and loading the dishwasher. I was happy to see the animals, especially my parakeet, Sunshine. Suddenly I could feel Ben's presence. When I told him about my bird, he had said, "*Sunshine*. That's a good name for you, too." I had laughed and asked him if he thought I should be in a cage.

Taylor actually purchased the little bird for me before we were married, just after my other parakeet died. Where had that considerate, caring person gone I wondered, trying to remember the last time he had bought me flowers or even a card. I changed into a nightgown and put on my new robe. It smelled like Ben. I hugged myself and took a deep breath as I walked out of the bathroom.

I found Taylor in the kitchen, leaning against the counter drinking a soda. When I asked him if anything was wrong, he said, "I have a lot on my mind."

"Well, is it business or personal? Why are you so quiet?" I couldn't help but ask, having just come home after two weeks in what would normally have been considered Hurricane Hell. He wasn't even going to hold me or make me a cup of tea? He wasn't even curious about my rescue?

"I have to go back to the office for a while. I'll talk to you when I get back. I won't be long. Do you need anything before I go?"

I shrugged and told him to do what he had to do. I nearly always told him that, but tonight should have been different. Then again, what made me think things would change just because I had survived a hurricane? We had been growing further apart since our wedding day, even more so since Taylor and Marcel started their business together. They had made it seem as though I'd be part of the company; but once I co-signed the loan papers for their new computers, it became clear that I was no longer needed. When I touted my accounting experience, I was informed that their amazing new software recorded every transaction, making bookkeeping obsolete.

Almost as soon as Taylor drove off, the phone rang. I was clearing my throat as I picked up the receiver. A voice said,

"Take another hit," then laughter, and then, "So, are you coming over or what?"

The voice was familiar. She was a friend of the guys, and according to the caller ID, she was calling from Marcel's place. I said, "Hello, Denise. Taylor just left, he should be there any minute."

I hung up before she could speak again. As my hand rested on the receiver, I began to understand why my husband had been so quiet. He had mentioned Denise a few times recently, but I had been under the impression that she was seeing Marcel. I never even considered that she might be interested in Taylor. That would explain the new clothes.

I wanted a glass of wine but there was none to be had, so I made a cup of tea and then dialed Dawn's number. She didn't sound surprised when I told her about Taylor going to the office. She had mentioned many times how disappointed she was in him, nearly as hurt as I was that he put on such a good show when he wanted to get married, then turning into such a slug... a word she loved to use. After she filled me in on which friends and family members she had called and the messages they asked her to give me, she put Kate on the phone.

"Hi Gram! I'm so glad you're safe. When are you coming to live with us?"

I wasn't quite prepared for her question; she had a way of cutting to the quick that sometimes caught me off guard, never failing to warm my heart with her honesty.

"I'll let you know, Angel. I have a few things to take care of first. How's school going? Are you the teacher's pet this year?"

Hearing her giggle always lifted my mood. She was constantly getting reprimanded for talking in class; the teacher's pet comment was a joke, one she quickly understood. Kate had a spirit that was endearing and she was usually very well behaved, but her spontaneous energy made it difficult to keep quiet in class. Dawn had done a wonderful job raising her, with absolutely no help from Kate's father whom she hadn't seen since she was a year old. Soon she'd be fourteen; where had the years gone? I couldn't wait to see my girls again.

After I hung up, I rearranged the flowers that PJ and Carrie sent. The card read, *Welcome Home, Mama. We Love You. P & C.*

I sniffed at a bright orange flower I'd never seen before. *What would I do without these kids?* I asked myself. There was a stack of unopened mail on the coffee table. I flipped through the pile and decided to leave it until tomorrow since it appeared to be mostly bills and junk mail. As I sat curled up on the sofa, Taylor's cat came out from her hiding place behind the piano and jumped up next to me. She sat purring as I brushed her fur and scratched her neck. "What's goin' on, Ruby? Did you miss me? It doesn't look like anyone else did."

After a few minutes the huge yellow cat with the strange red dot between her eyes, jumped down and went to her food dish. Ants were crawling on the food, and she looked up at me as if to say, "See what I've had to put up with?"

I dumped her food into the sink, then cleaned her dish and refilled it. I wiped up the floor and rinsed the ants down the drain as I turned on the garbage disposal. The grinding noise reminded me of the sound the rescue boat had made. I smiled thinking about our trip to the clinic, and how wonderful it felt to have Ben's arms around me. Even when the boat stalled, I wasn't afraid. I picked up the phone and dialed his number, warmed and soothed by the sound of his voice on the answering machine.

"Hi, this is Ben. If you're looking for Nicole, call Long Island. If you're looking for me, please leave a message after the beep."

I closed my eyes and smiled, picturing him getting my message when he came home.

Suddenly there was a scratch at the back door and I turned around to see our dog, Coco. She was a mongrel, part Lab and part Terrier, given to us by some friends who moved to a condo that didn't allow pets. I hadn't wanted a dog but Taylor insisted that we take her, saying that she'd make a great watchdog. Her nose was pushed flat against the glass, and I smiled as I walked toward the door. She was seldom allowed inside because of the dirt and fleas she brought in with her. Once a beautiful green lawn, the backyard had become a dried-out, sandy, insect-infested eyesore.

"What the hell. Come on in, girl," I said as I opened the door. She smelled terrible, badly in need of a bath. I winced as she shook her body, bits of sand and debris flying about the room. I decided it might be time for Taylor's parents to take her; they had offered several times. Even though he insisted on keeping the dog, Taylor never walked her and seldom took care of her. She had grown too big for me to bathe or walk. I was no longer strong enough to hang on to her leash and it hurt my back to keep up with her. But she was a sweet dog, craving attention from anyone who would give it to her.

"Poor Coco," I said as I led her back outside to the patio and filled her water bowl. The food dish was half full, so I assumed she had eaten. Either that or the dog didn't like ants any more than the cat did. She whined and tried to follow me as I walked inside and closed the door.

Taylor came home about two hours later. I didn't mention Denise's call, but he did. "Sorry I took so long. Marcel, Denise and I were taking turns in an online chess tournament. She said she called here. I hadn't told them you'd be home today."

"Why not? Did you forget? It seems kind of funny that you would enter a chess tournament on my first day back, after the hurricane and being injured and all. You sure have a strange way of showing concern, and of course you have the football game tomorrow. Anyway, I'm tired so I'm going to bed."

He told me again that he was sorry, that they had registered before he knew when I was coming home. Then he sat down at his desk and switched on his computer.

I went into the guest room, now my room, and lay down on the bed. I wasn't sure what to do. I had left a message for Ben, telling him about my strange homecoming, and that I would call him back when I got the chance. He should be home by now since he lived just over three hours from Orlando. I missed him so much, but I was glad that we hadn't made love. That would only have complicated things further, and whatever was happening here was enough for me to deal with right now. I felt sad and numb, as though I had been forced awake from a most pleasant dream.

Something was definitely wrong. The guilt that crept into my thoughts on the drive home was gone, giving way to something far more disturbing. I wasn't sure what was going on, but I suspected it had something to do with Denise. I had been shaking inside since her call, realizing that I may have turned a blind eye to trouble lurking in the shadows. But, why bother checking out the shadows when there was already trouble in the light.

I decided to get up and talk to Taylor. I would make more tea and try to get to the bottom of all this mystery. At first he didn't want to talk, but I insisted. Obviously something had happened while I was away, and he needed to tell me about it. Putting things off until tomorrow wouldn't work for me.

He finally submitted to my urgings, and started to talk. He told me that he and Denise had gotten closer since Marcel met a new female friend through some online chat room. The three of them were good friends. Denise had been spending more time at Marcel's since she finished her last modeling gig. She was having trouble finding work, so they had offered her a job.

I interrupted. "You guys can't even pay yourselves, yet you're hiring her. To do what exactly?"

Denise was from Granada, a real beauty. I didn't know she wasn't modeling anymore. My chest muscles tightened as I waited for an answer. I remembered Taylor telling me once that he was much more trustworthy than other men, but that all men were animals, for the most part.

I didn't speak again as he talked. He ignored my question about Denise working for the company. Instead, he told me again that he was sorry and that he would stop seeing her; but that I should understand how lost he was sometimes, that he needed me to help him. I didn't know if he was confused or whether I just didn't get the point he was trying to make. He became quite animated when he started talking about all the times I had gone to visit my sister.

"Over a dozen times in less than three years," he reminded me emphatically.

"That may have seemed extreme," I agreed. "But she was dying, what was I supposed to do?"

He looked at me with tears in his eyes and said, "A man has needs."

I don't know why that sounded so funny, but I started laughing. I laughed until I cried and I just kept crying. Taylor patted me on my back, a feigned gesture that I had always hated. I picked up my arm and gently pushed him away. This didn't have to get nasty—it just had to get over. I asked him to leave, for good. I told him I understood, that I could accept this, and that I didn't want to go on the way we were anyway. We had nothing in common anymore. He wasn't interested in me or in what I wanted, and quite honestly I felt the same way about him. We had long since stopped being happy. Our marriage was never a true partnership, and now we could stop the charade.

"In fact," I added, "I was planning to leave soon."

Taylor stared down at the floor while I talked, not bothering to disagree. He just kept saying he was sorry, sort of mumbling and shaking his head. He looked up when I finished speaking.

"You were planning to leave? When were you going to tell me?"

I slowly shook my head, not bothering to answer him. I wondered how long he and Denise had been in love. They were providing me with a convenient way out of a bad situation. It seemed too good to be true, and yet it didn't feel all that good right now. Taylor finished stuffing clothes into his duffle bag and then looked down at me as if he were waiting to be dismissed.

"It's okay, Taylor. I understand. I honestly do understand." I took his hand and gave it a light squeeze as he started toward the door.

I sat on my bed and stared out the window into the atrium. The light was shining on the huge porcelain fountain that I kept after closing my store nearly ten years earlier. The sculptural piece was the work of an incredible artist, Peter Wendland, made on Mendon Mountain in Vermont. It needed cleaning—the motor was clogged and the water no longer flowed easily over the rocks. Eventually I stopped shaking and realized that

I was thinking about a malfunctioning fountain instead of the fact that my marriage had just ended.

It seemed late to call Ben but I knew he'd be anxious to hear from me. I could hear the smile in his voice when he answered. He was wide-awake, waiting for my call.

"I'm so sorry you had to go through that, Sweetheart, but I have to admit that the news makes me happy. Let me come over. I can leave right away; I've already mapped it out."

"No, Ben. It's too late, and too dangerous to drive Alligator Alley at night. I'd rather you wait until next weekend, actually. I need some time to let everything sink in. I know it's the best thing that could have happened, but it came as a real shock. It all happened so fast, and I'm still too stunned to think straight. I'm relieved, and blown away, and hurt, all at once."

I took a deep breath and heard him do the same. "Thank you for being there for me, Ben. I miss you so much. I'll call you tomorrow and we can make plans for the weekend. Okay? Let's both try to get some sleep."

"Okay, Angel, I'll talk to you tomorrow. Everything will work out fine, I promise. Thank you so much for calling me." He kissed me through the phone before he hung up.

"Night, Ben. Thank you... for everything."

I felt happy to have heard his voice, relieved to know that I would hear it again tomorrow, and the next day, and always. After I hung up, I felt drained, so weak and tired that I could hardly stand up. I slumped down on my bed and held my head in my hands for what seemed like hours, thoughts swirling through my head like a tornado. I had spent two weeks dreaming about being with Ben, and wishing that Taylor would find someone else. Now that it had happened, I felt disillusioned and confused. I was glad that Ben agreed to wait a few days before coming over. It would take a while to adjust to what had happened, and to get used to the idea of another divorce.

Falling asleep seemed more like passing out, and I woke a few hours later wondering if I had dreamed it all. Fully awake, I realized that the shock and confusion were real—Taylor was gone. I didn't know whether I had been psychic once again, or whether I might have willed this to happen.

I drifted off to sleep again and dreamed about the hurricane. Ben had gone outside against my wishes. I waited and waited, afraid of the noise and of being alone. Things were crashing into the trailer, and I couldn't stop my leg from bleeding. I woke to the sound of the telephone ringing.

"Hello," I shouted.

"Mom, are you all right? What's wrong? Did I wake you?"

"I'm fine, Honey. I was just having a bad dream. Everything's okay, depending on how you look at it. Taylor's gone."

I told her briefly about Denise and promised to call her back after I had my coffee. I needed to clear the cobwebs from my brain and put it to work. I had loads of work to do, and many decisions to make.

As I stumbled to the bathroom, I thought about Ben making coffee on the grill. My God, how I missed him.

Chapter 10

Going Home

Ben decided not to buy my brother's property, of course, since neither of us wanted to live in Florida. Yet I discovered that I no longer detested the state; it was where I'd found Ben, after all. He would arrange to have the trailer cleaned out and get the land cleared, and Mr. Minton offered to negotiate a sale to the realtor who had made the best offer. The net proceeds would be deposited into a trust fund for Trudy, which he would oversee. I felt relieved that I didn't have to return to the trailer, even though it held so many fond memories.

Less than a week had passed since I last saw Ben, and each day I missed him more. Our daily phone calls helped me stay balanced as I sorted through boxes and drawers, cleaned out closets and cupboards, and prepared for my departure. Taylor and I spoke several times, about the business and finances, how to get my name off the company debts, and how to tell his relatives that we had split. Few of our friends would be surprised, not that we had many in common. His parents would be the ones hardest to tell. I suggested he tell them that they had lost a daughter-in-law, but that they could have the dog. He didn't laugh.

My attorney called to inform me that the insurance company had finally agreed to settle my personal injury claim, with an offer more than triple their first one. Even after legal expenses and surgery, I'd have enough to live on for several years. What a relief not to have to endure a trial. Selling my house was next on the agenda. It was mortgaged to its value, so there would be little profit from the sale. Money, however, was not at the forefront of my mind. Love and happiness began to fill my psyche, melting away many years of anger and depression. When Ben called on Thursday night, I told him my good news and suggested that we spend the weekend near the ocean.

He sounded happy and excited. "The beach is a great idea. I'll make reservations and drive over Saturday morning. I'm desperate to see you."

"Me, too," I said, kissing him through the phone and giggling as I hung up.

I felt energized by the thought of seeing Ben, filled with anticipation but not at all nervous, possibly for the first time in my life. He made the situation seem more like a chance for happiness and less like an outrageous failure. The weekend would allow us to reconnect on a whole new level. Two more days in paradise, without guilt, and free to be together in any way we chose.

The hotel was located on Hallandale Beach, just south of Fort Lauderdale near Alligator Alley. Easy to find and convenient for both of us, a short taxi ride for me. I sat in the lobby reading a newspaper as I waited for Ben to arrive, quickly rising to greet him when he walked in.

He smiled when he saw me and said, "Hi, Baby," as he put down his bag to give me a big hug and a real kiss. After he checked in, we headed to our room, holding hands and talking, both smiling ear to ear. Several other people stepped onto the elevator, and Ben gave me a look that seemed to say, *It's a good thing they're here.* His suggestive look made me laugh; I could feel my cheeks getting red. As soon as the door to the room was open, he shoved our bags into the closet, taking me into his arms as he closed the door. We kissed and laughed as we pulled each other's clothes off, not quite like teenagers in heat but with a passion I had never known before. There didn't seem to be any change in how we felt about each other, no apprehension or fear of commitment, on his part or mine.

We spent the afternoon talking, laughing, and indulging each other's whims. With some gentle persuasion on my part, Ben divulged that he had always fantasized about having someone feed him grapes, while fanning him with a feather. As a young boy, he admired a painting depicting a similar scene. Since I didn't have a feather, I used the paper mat from under the ice bucket, folding it neatly into a fan. I separated the grapes that were left over from our lunch and placed them in a napkin on my pillow. He looked completely at ease as he lay on the bed watching me with a huge smile on his face, taking full advantage of my willingness to please him.

As I popped the last grape into his mouth, he pouted. "Ah, no grapes left for you. How on earth shall I please you?"

"I fancy having my hair brushed and my nails polished, please, Sir." When he scowled at the nail polish, I added, "Pardon me, whose fancy is this, anyway? And did I not indulge you in an extra little delight while I was feeding you grapes? Nearly caused you to pass out, if I remember correctly."

My Southern Belle accent made him laugh, and he slowly opened the bottle. The polish was clear so he didn't make too much mess, but it was obvious that he had never given anyone a manicure. Afterwards, he massaged my back and we made love again. We would have missed the sunset if Ben hadn't noticed a golden glow through the drapes on the westward side of the hotel. We threw on our clothes and went for a walk on the beach.

"Sunsets are the nicest part of living on the gulf coast of Florida," Ben said as we walked.

I couldn't think of a single thing other than the ocean that I liked about the east coast, until he was here. I knew that living in a tropical climate would have been far more enjoyable if I could have spent that time with someone like Ben. He told me that he had to stop himself from planning out our life, after I called to tell him about Taylor and Denise. He wanted us to plan our future together, he couldn't wait to start, and he would be happy any place that I was.

"I hope you like green mountains," I said as I tightened my arm around his waist. I could only hope he meant what he said.

From the smile on his face and his returned hug, I felt pretty sure that both his intentions and his words were true.

The setting sun honored us with a breathtaking display of orange and pink clouds, purple rays slicing through the billowy masses and promising yet another glorious day. The hurricane seemed like a distant memory. As we walked back toward our hotel we stepped into the water and held each other, feeling the wind, and listening to the shore birds and the waves. Ben's lips tasted salty as they brushed softly against mine. Our backs were toward the ocean as we stood staring at the incredible sky. Suddenly a huge wave splashed us, soaking us to above our waists. Laughing and running, we headed back to our room. After a few yards, my legs and my back reminded me that I don't run. Funny the things you forget when you're in love.

Still dripping wet when we reached our room, Ben started my bath while I peeled off my wet clothes. We agreed on room service again, and he brought me the menu and a glass of chardonnay as I slipped into the hot water. I asked if he would like to join me, surprised by how easily the question came to mind. The modesty I always felt when naked or even partially exposed, no longer seemed to be there. Perhaps that phobia would vanish, like so many of my qualms and inhibitions that all seemed to subside effortlessly when I was with Ben. He had a way of looking at me with pure love in his eyes, never judging or condescending, making me feel special and without flaws. Through four marriages and several so-called love affairs, no one had ever provided the respect and adoration that my wounded ego craved.

The evening was spectacular. Not like fireworks on the 4th of July or a gala Broadway production; this was far better—a romantic vacation with a beautiful man who was now my lover and my intended life partner. All of my senses seemed heightened and I felt like the luckiest woman on earth.

The lobster rolls we ordered were messy but delicious. We wet our napkins with mineral water to wipe the drips off each other's chins and chests, delighted at our sloppiness and appetites. The ocean air smelled fresh, lacking the strong odor of salt and seaweed that had been evident on the west coast, just before the storm. We left our balcony door open, the shutters on each side providing plenty of privacy. Our room was on the third floor, with the ocean just yards away. We could hear the surf, the seagulls and little else as we leaned against the railing sipping sparkling water and enjoying the breeze. As nightfall approached, the lights along A1A reflected rainbow colors in the surf as it washed languidly over the sand.

Sunday morning arrived with feelings of wonderment, waking up next to each other for the first time, under the same covers, naked. Ben touched my thigh as I climbed out of bed to go to the bathroom. When I returned, he rolled over and pulled me close to him. We made love as though we had been together always. For the first time in my life, I felt only happiness.

Like most of our days together, Sunday proved to be a joyous one, filled with laughter and pleasant discoveries. We enjoyed each other's company and each other's bodies. Ben was very strong and well in control of his muscles; there was never a clumsy movement or an awkward moment. He didn't treat me like a china doll yet he was very careful not to hurt me. I felt pampered and safe, at ease in any position, and unaware of the outside world.

We lay sprawled on the bed massaging each other's feet as we talked. Ben said, "I wanted so much to do these things while we were stranded in the trailer, to be close to you and take care of you in every way, to let you know how I felt about you."

"Oh Ben, you did so many things during that time that showed me how you felt. I've never been so well cared for, and I've absolutely never met anyone like you, not even close. I love everything about you—your touch, your smell, the way you look, the way you walk."

"Stop it, Sunshine. You'll give me a big head," he laughed. "You know I feel the same about you, though. You're the best thing that ever happened to me. You want to be my girl?"

"I think I already am," I said as I touched the diamond earrings he had given me on Saturday.

He handed me the box shortly after we made love for the first time. "These belonged to my mother and I want you to have them. I know she'd want me to give them to you. They were a gift from my father."

Tears fell from my eyes as I thanked him. The earrings were precious, small and tasteful, not at all flashy. I knew how much they must mean to him. The fact that he wanted me to have something that his dear mother treasured, that his own father had given her, meant more to me than anything I could imagine. The gesture left me unable to speak. We stayed quiet in each other's arms for several minutes before I placed them in my ears.

On Sunday afternoon, Ben suggested that we visit an upscale boutique that he spotted from the boardwalk the day before. He helped me pick out several flattering dresses, comfortable and not too fussy, a bathing suit, and another sarong skirt. Buying things for me brought him great pleasure, he said, pointing out that my clothes didn't really fit anymore. I had lost nearly fifteen pounds since we first met, and I was looking "mighty fine," or so he told me. His compliments and tenderness made me feel young and pretty. I hadn't felt that way in years; in fact I had never felt that way even when I *was* young and pretty. I wasn't at all accustomed to being treated so well.

Ben never hesitated when I asked him to do something, whether it meant getting dressed to go downstairs for ice or to the car for a forgotten item. Taylor's habit of procrastinating had long since stopped me from asking him to do anything. Even asking for Ben's help took some getting used to, but he made it easy. Whenever he saw me doing something that he could do, he would simply stop me and take over. Whether I started drawing a bath or moving a chair, he insisted that I let him help me. He didn't just pay lip service by saying, "I would have helped, why didn't you ask me?"

I had called Taylor earlier that day from a payphone in the lobby. I asked if he had finished moving his belongings out of the house. "Partially," he answered. No surprise there since I hadn't seen him meet a deadline since our wedding day.

"Well, I'll stay here another night, and whatever you leave in the house will get put in boxes and donated to charity. I've decided to put the house on the market right away, and I plan to leave the state as soon as it's sold."

He sounded indignant. "Couldn't you wait a while? I could take over the mortgage; maybe my parents would co-sign for me."

"Uh, no. That's not going to happen." I reminded him that the house was mine long before we married, and as he had argued many times, it was mortgaged to its value. Since he had seldom made a house payment during the years we'd been together, there was no need to debate the issue. The house belonged to me. I didn't mention that I had already spoken to a realtor or that my lawsuit had been settled. It would be a month or so before the money came through, and I hoped to be in Vermont soon after that.

Ben drove me home Monday afternoon. He carried my bags inside, and checked out the house as if he were a potential buyer. His face registered disbelief as he scanned the neglected back yard, looking up at the water stains on the ceilings as he stepped back into the house. He kept his opinions to himself, but I noticed him shaking his head a few times. I felt sure he could see that my contempt for Taylor's laziness wasn't just in my mind. Very little effort had been put into the property in recent years.

Instead of driving home, Ben returned to the hotel room and called to suggest that we go to dinner. He had decided to leave the next morning and couldn't see any reason why we should spend the night apart. His call delighted me, and I decided it was the perfect occasion to wear one of my new dresses. The soft pima cotton material felt like silk against my skin, draping loosely from my shoulders to my knees. As I brushed my hair, I noticed the sparkle of my diamond earrings dancing in the mirror, and I smiled at the thought of his love and generosity. The mirror smiled back at me as I whispered, "I love you, Ben."

By the time my date arrived, I had great news to share. I had listed the house just four days earlier. That afternoon, my realtor called to ask if he could show the house. Shortly before Ben returned to pick me up, the realtor came by with a potential buyer who had been looking for a house in my neighborhood. Despite the home's condition, the buyer loved the property and signed the contract on my dining room table. The house needed work and therefore priced below market value, causing the motivated young man to jump at what he saw as an excellent investment opportunity. The sale would net enough to pay both the mortgage and equity loans, and the realtor's fee, with about two thousand dollars to spare. Not much profit for having owned the house for over ten years, but all that was needed. The contract called for a closing in thirty days.

Ben and I celebrated with a glass of champagne and the chef's surf and turf special: crab stuffed lobster tail and petite filet mignon. We agreed that we had never enjoyed a meal more, and we talked about eating there again one day as we returned to our room at the hotel. After we made love, we talked long into the night. The next day Ben returned to work and gave his notice to Mr. Minton. He would be leaving after his caseload was cleared, and planned to join me in Vermont as soon as that happened. His boss sadly accepted his resignation, which hadn't come as any surprise. Mr. Minton had encouraged our relationship, often mentioning that he'd never seen Ben so happy. Even though he was losing his favorite employee, he wanted only the best for us.

It took the entire month to clean out the house. I couldn't believe how much unnecessary stuff had accumulated during the time I'd lived in that house. Taylor and I were both packrats. My friend Valerie brought boxes and helped me pack and clean the house. Val was the only true friend who remained from where I had worked. She resigned shortly after I left, finding another job and returning to college part-time to earn her teaching certificate.

Hired to replace Nancy, Val never grew to like the position. She was appalled at the way our bosses blew money and by how quickly their loyalties changed after my accident. Once I was gone, she couldn't stand being there. Valerie was one of the smartest, most interesting and lovely women I'd ever met, her long auburn hair scrunched up on her head, with wire rim glasses perched on her nose in an obvious attempt to look scholarly instead of pretty. I offered her the job within five minutes of meeting her, dozens of other applicants having been turned away. Now, without her help, I would never have been able to accomplish the overwhelming task of cleaning up the past ten years of my life. We would miss each other greatly, but she knew I had to go and she was thrilled that Taylor was out of my life. She had watched me struggle along without his help, fuming mad at his lack of concern. Val was younger than my daughter, yet we were the closest of friends. Her infectious laughter had lifted me from many somber moods.

My attorney referred me to a brilliant neurosurgeon in North Miami. Dr. Kenneth Lusgarten had an impeccable reputation, and had reviewed all of my medical records. I would be in the best of hands, and since my claim was settled, there was no need to endure the pain any longer. The broken disc between my third and fourth lumbar vertebrae was pinching my sciatic nerve. Surgery would involve such procedures as discectomy, hemilaminectomy, facetectomy, and lysis of nerve root adhesions. The words sounded frightening, but all were fairly common procedures. It had been nearly three years since my accident, and at times the pain was unbearable. Even though I hated taking the strong medications that were prescribed, I could barely function without them anymore. My doctor appeared confident that the surgery would eliminate the need for pills, and that I would make a full recovery. The process would take time, patience, and determination. I told him I was up to the challenge.

Ben felt terrible that he couldn't be there to care for me. He had taken one last case as a favor to Mr. Minton, the court date already scheduled; there was no getting out of it. I assured him that I would be fine and that having him in my heart was almost as good as having him by my side. Val brought me to the hospital at five-thirty in the morning on one of her rare days off, and she would bring me home with her after I was released. She and her husband, Scott had prepared their guest room for me and many boxes of my belongings were already stashed in their garage. Dawn planned to fly down the following week and take me home to Vermont to recuperate.

The surgery went well, although the morphine nearly killed me. Most of the pain was gone almost immediately, and I could walk without help within a week. Ben called several times each day, proud of me for managing so well without him. I felt like I could handle anything; downright ecstatic that my surgery was over, my house was sold, and my case was settled. And Ben loved me.

Soon I was back in my beloved Green Mountain state, near my girls, with money in the bank. Ben's case finally went to court but ended up in appeal, taking nearly two more months to finalize. Our daily phone calls were filled with discussion about the political mess in Florida, the fight over who had won the election, the never-ending debates over voting regulations, and the tedious and ambiguous counting of hanging 'chads' on the voting ballots. We laughed at the absurdity but were saddened by how costly the process had become, and about how all that money could have been used to feed the hungry and help conquer disease.

Most of my time was spent doing the back-strengthening exercises that my surgeon outlined. Feeling so strong mentally made the healing process easier, and staying with the girls kept me from feeling lonely. They made me feel welcome and appreciated for the simple chores I did, for the meals I prepared, and most especially, for coming home.

Between court dates, Ben flew to Vermont twice. Thanksgiving day was his first time meeting the girls. The visit was short, only three days, but we all had a wonderful time. Ben and Kate hit it off right away, after he threw a snowball at her, just skimming the edge of her boot. Hearing her screams and giggles as she basted him with snowballs, had Dawn and me roaring with laughter. Instead of trying to avoid her throws, he kept trying to catch them. The next day he helped her build a snowman. After Ben left, Kate told me that she had never had so much fun with any guy, except for her uncle PJ.

On his second visit, Ben arrived on Christmas Eve and stayed for ten days. He brought very thoughtful gifts for the girls: a *Walkman* for Kate and a *Palm Pilot* for Dawn. Kate had learned to crochet, and the scarf she made for him, using seven shades of gray yarn, brought tears to his eyes. He and I exchanged the Victorian sterling buckle rings we found at an antique shop on his previous visit, as tokens of our love and commitment to each other.

As he placed the ring on my finger, he smiled and said, "I now pronounce us *buckled*." From that day on, he referred to me as his wife and told me to let him know if I ever wanted to make it official. We started 2001 together and promised each other that we would be together always. He dreaded returning to Florida but he said he would never leave Mr. Minton hanging. He knew he'd win the appeal; it was just a formality, but a painstaking one, nonetheless.

"It will be nice to go out with a win," he said. "Mostly, though, I just want to do a good job for Mr. Minton. He's always treated me like a son."

Having grown fond of Mr. Minton myself, I didn't complain. I felt grateful for his support and the kindness he showed my brother, and me. Ben would soon be joining me for good. We would just need to be patient a little longer. We had waited all our lives to find each other; a few more weeks wouldn't kill us. One thing seemed certain to both of us, absence really does make hearts grow stronger. Before Ben left for the final time, we found a small apartment where we would live when he returned, while looking for a house or some land to build on. With four rooms and a nice large bath, it would suit us fine.

Dawn and Kate helped me furnish the apartment, mostly with donated items from friends and relatives. Even though I could now afford to buy whatever I wanted, it didn't make sense to spend a bunch of money on a temporary rental. Ben opened a joint checking account for us, and he told me to use whatever I needed. I used only one check, for the deposit on the apartment. He insisted on that even though my own bank account now showed a healthy balance, with the remainder of the settlement tucked away in mutual funds.

The girls and I had great fun decorating the place, making it feel cozy and warm. They were thrilled to have me living only seven miles away. It warmed my heart to see how happy it made them, and I was sorry that I had been so far away for too many years. I would need to forgive myself that, and for all the other mistakes I'd made. Ben and I were starting a new life, and I didn't want to bring along any unnecessary baggage. He talked to me about letting go of our pasts.

As he put it, "Babe, we have each other now. Let's forget about Taylor, and Nicole, and all the other losers in our lives. It's time for us to be happy. You have a wonderful family, and all I want is to be a part of it."

If Ben could accept my past, then so could I. Feelings of love and gratitude filled my heart while I waited for his return, determined to gain the strength to be a healthy and helpful companion. The New England winter was harsh so I stayed inside most of the time, nearly wearing out the carpets striding back and forth because my doctor had called walking "the best exercise in the world." He also warned me of the damage I could do if I injured myself while I was healing, not at all pleased that I chose to move to a place with so much ice.

Ben finally finished his work at the law office and returned for good in February, just in time for Valentine's Day. He insisted on cooking us dinner, something he hadn't been able to do since the hurricane. As the lamb chops sizzled on the broiler, he prepared couscous and asparagus, explaining each step as if he were broadcasting his own cooking show. I laughed and asked him if he'd been watching the food network.

"Just call me Emeril," he joked.

For dessert we ate chocolate truffles from a local bakery and sipped raspberry brandy in front of the gas fireplace that had coaxed us into renting the apartment. The fireplace had provided me with much needed ambiance during all those cold nights alone. I felt blessed to be spending Valentines Day in such a romantic setting with the man I loved. I thought about karma and how the universe really does provide. Sometimes it just takes a while.

Ben adjusted quickly to the cold weather. He had missed living in the north; said he took the job in Florida to get as far away from Long Island as possible. Soon he was wearing flannel shirts under his parka and wool socks under his boots. My Yankee had finally made his way home, excited about all the winter activities that Vermont offered. Dawn gave him a ski pass, one of the perks she received for being the office manager at the local ski association. We hoped I might be able to ski with him next winter, maybe even go skating.

My brother-in-law invited Ben to go ice fishing one weekend. I made them both promise that they wouldn't go too far out on the ice.

Ben smiled as he started out the door behind Dave, then walked back to me and said, "Don't worry, Sunshine. You won't get rid of me that easily." He gave me a long hug, then asked my sister to keep me off chairs while he was gone.

Claire had already busied herself attaching rings to the curtains we planned to hang. She looked up at Ben and laughed. "I'll try, but no promises. You know how she is."

Our lives merged easily into a natural pattern of family, friends, and fun. It seemed like we had always been together; I felt convinced that we should have been. Spring came with a blast of flowers and warm air. Ben's love, along with the delightful weather, helped me heal completely. We went for walks every day, rain or shine, and my back grew stronger with each step. My life was happier than I ever dreamed it could be. Ben was always there for me yet he never hovered over me, respecting my independence and allowing me to take care of myself, now that I could.

He encouraged me to write, always anxious to review my work, and praising me constantly. I no longer wrote for therapy, instead I wrote when I felt like writing or to pass the time when Ben was gone. He didn't like being *under foot,* a term his Mom had always used for hanging around and doing *nothing.* He joined the local tennis club, playing tennis with anyone who needed a partner. I sometimes watched him play; always impressed by his strength and physique, happy to know he would be sharing my bed that night. When I sat courtside, he would wink at me and smile, clearly pleased to have me nearby.

My friends Roy and Sally became Ben's friends as well. Two of my dearest friends, they were a remarkable couple, the type whose family was more important than social status and whose door was always open to me. We had become friends while I worked briefly as their bookkeeper before I started my contracting business, and we had remained friends through all sorts of troubles, both theirs and mine.

Once a week, Ben and Roy played golf, and they talked about going to hockey games next winter at Norwich University, Roy's alma mater. Sally and I shared many bottles of wine together over the twenty plus years we were friends. Their house was always my favorite place to visit before I moved to Florida, and whenever I came back to Vermont to help my sister and see my family. My friends were delighted that I returned home, and that I had finally found happiness with this terrific guy named Ben.

Nearly every weekend Ben and I roamed through flea markets and antique shops. We went out to eat or to listen to a band at least once a week, often inviting Roy and Sally or Dawn and Kate to join us for dinner. Kate invariably ordered chicken fingers, and Ben teased her about turning into a hen someday. She told him not to worry about it since he and I hadn't turned into fish yet. Their banter was always entertaining.

Ben decided to use the summer months to relax and contemplate a career change. He mentioned starting a small law office to help people who couldn't otherwise afford legal help. It might be nice to be a country lawyer like his father instead of defending big city corporations, "the fats" as he referred to his former clients. I suggested that he take his time and seriously consider whether he wanted to practice law; he seemed set against that while he was in Florida. Once we found a place where we wanted to live, he could make up his mind about what to do. There was no hurry.

We combed the local papers for the perfect house or parcel of land, often driving around the countryside envisioning our dream property, which could be just around the next corner. Few nice homes or building lots came on the market in our immediate area. Even in a state where cows outnumber people, the housing and land shortage was becoming a problem. We loved our apartment, so it didn't really matter how long it took to find what we were looking for. In fact, we had so much fun looking that we passed up several possibilities. We were happy and in no rush, convinced that the universe would provide the right home in time; we had the rest of our lives to look, to laugh, and to love each other.

Chapter 11

Life Goes On

Summer seemed to fly by, with fall starting to make its appearance by the middle of August. Nights grew colder, and mornings held the chill while waiting to be warmed by the midday sun. Spots of color adorned the hillsides, announcing the brilliance that was yet to come. Round bales of hay were scattered throughout pastures as farmers readied their fields and livestock for the approaching winter. The days were getting shorter, little by little. Ben and I felt excited about spending our first autumn together in New England. Enchanted by quaint villages where we found interesting antique shops and small restaurants that offered home cooking and friendly conversation, we knew the foliage would only enhance their charm.

Our drives took us throughout the county and beyond. Ben loved the countryside near the town where I was raised, often driving the back roads in Calais, Woodbury, or Adamant. He said the area reminded him of where he grew up. On one of our many rides over back roads, he pulled into the driveway of the very house in Maple Corner where I was born. I had pointed it out once or twice, commenting that it looked much different than I remembered.

"Whatcha doin,' Hon?" I asked through my smile.

"Just want to see who lives here now," he answered.

I actually knew who lived there, and that the property wasn't likely to be for sale, but I didn't say anything. Instead, I watched him approach the front door as I sat in the Land Rover remembering the little girl I once was, and the pony that was my favorite of all the animals on the farm. My big brother Donald named the pony Superman, after my father had taken it as payment for a debt. I was too little to ride by myself, so Don gave me rides, holding the reins while I hung onto the saddle horn. I thought about what a shame it was that Don died so young, in his early thirties, leaving a wife and three kids. I was glad that we had stopped, and that our impromptu visit had evoked such fond memories of my brother.

No one was home. Ben returned to the car looking slightly disappointed. I told him I didn't think the house was right for us anyway, too big and a little too far from the girls. He sighed and nodded his head in agreement, apparently as sentimental about my youth as he was about his own. He often talked about going fishing and camping with his Dad, and how his Mom helped them get ready for their adventures by packing their favorite foods and making sure they packed the right clothes. She usually stayed home to watch the pets and catch up on her sewing and paperwork. Her allergies kept her from participating in many outdoor activities, but she never objected to her husband and son enjoying their "guy stuff," as she called it. I could tell that Ben still missed them both very much. I wished I had known them and that Ben had known my mother.

We made plans to drive to New York over the Labor Day weekend. Ben was anxious to show me his land; he hoped we could have a second home there one day. He also wanted to meet with the attorney who executed his parent's will and handled his trust fund, which he hadn't touched in all these years.

Fall was the perfect time of year to take the ferry across Lake Champlain, to enjoy the colorful views together like we dreamed about when we were stranded during the hurricane. First we would visit his childhood home and walk his land, or as much as we could cover of the sixty-five acres. From there we would drive to Manhattan to visit his friends. Then he would meet with his attorney to sign the trust papers before returning home. We wanted to be back in time to celebrate Kate's fifteenth birthday and to watch her first field hockey game of the season. It was her second year on the junior varsity team. Ben bought her a new stick and had coached her at home. He said he couldn't wait to see her in action.

Kate spent part of the summer in Florida with her grandfather, and Ben talked about how much he missed her while she was gone. In such a short period of time, Kate had grown from a precocious little girl into a charming, poised young lady. Yet she was still a child in so many ways, never having lost her ability to have fun. It filled my heart with joy to see Ben with the girls. Whenever we visited, he would help Kate with homework, play a game with her, or take her on errands. He often made minor repairs at their house or washed Dawn's car. He loved being outside, and it was his nature to stay busy and be helpful. Neither of my girls or my son grew up with a father; now we all had Ben.

PJ and Carrie were planning to visit us in October. I hadn't seen my son and daughter-in-law in over a year. I felt elated that they were coming and that they would finally get to meet Ben. They had been married for nearly five years but still acted like newlyweds, happy as children and a joy to be around. I had no doubt that Ben would love them as dearly as he already loved our girls. Kate adored her aunt, and her uncle was her hero. Seeing the way my children interacted, the way my daughter and my daughter-in-law had grown to be the best of friends, made me very proud to be their mother. Dawn and PJ had grown closer once they became adults, and they both showed their appreciation for how they were raised. I didn't give myself much credit during those years, but the people my kids became proved that I had done something right.

Shortly after we made our plans to visit New York, I started experiencing severe chest pains. Sleep, when it finally came, brought nightmares and more discomfort. The pain felt similar to the anxiety attacks I had in Florida, when my life was crazy and stressful. There was no reason to be feeling any anxiety now since my life was relaxed and filled with happiness. I thought the pain might be a recurrence of the pericarditis that I suffered many years earlier, caused by anemia. I refused to go to the emergency room, but Ben insisted that I see a doctor. After nearly a week with no improvement, I agreed to go. Not that Ben was planning to take no for an answer—he said he'd carry me over his shoulder if he had to. Knowing my family's medical history, Dawn worried about my heart. Both of my parents, and my younger sister, died from heart disease.

I went through a series of tests, all indicating that my heart was healthy. Blood tests determined that I was not anemic. Ultimately my doctor decided that the pain might be from an inflamed esophagus or other gastric problems, prescribing medication to try and instructing me to rest. The tests were inconclusive; all I could do was take the medicine and wait to see if it helped. I was relieved that the problem didn't appear to be with my heart, although my chest hurt constantly and I had trouble breathing. The mystery of my insomnia went unsolved, and terrifying nightmares continued to plague my nights.

Ben rescheduled his trip for the weekend after Labor Day. He would go alone this time, and we would travel to New York together another time. He wanted to transfer the trust funds to his money market account so the money would be available when we found the right property. I hated for him to go without me, but my doctor warned me that riding and sitting upright for any length of time would only exacerbate my condition. I tried to overlook my fears, hoping that my nightmares were not some form of premonition. Ben assured me that he would make it a fast trip—four days, tops. I asked why he couldn't just do things by mail, trying not to seem possessive while expressing my concerns. His gentle, tolerant answer made me feel bad for questioning him.

"I really want to get the rest of my Mom's jewelry out of the safe deposit box, and my Dad's army medals from his tour in Korea. It will be nice to have them with me; I haven't looked at them in years. Everything will be fine, Sweetie, and all this worry will seem silly once I return."

As much as I still didn't want him to go, it seemed selfish to ask him to change his plans again. So I helped him plan his trip and even tried to pretend that I was looking forward to having some time alone, trying not to let my anxiety show. There was no way to hide my vivid nightmares of fires and explosions. Each time I woke up crying, Ben would hold me and reassure me that there was nothing to be afraid of. He would be driving his trusty Land Rover so the dreams couldn't possibly suggest danger for him; there was clearly nothing to worry about. He wrote down numbers for all the people he would be seeing: his realtor, his friends, and his attorney.

He planned to leave on Friday morning and would meet with his friend Logan who was a realtor, on Saturday, to arrange to have his land appraised. He said he'd never sell it, but we could always use it for collateral on a mortgage if needed. He didn't want to disappoint his friends by canceling again, so he would drive into the city on Sunday and spend Monday with them. He had known them since he was in pre-med with Laurie, and the couple had become like family after his parents died.

Dawn offered to stay with me until Ben returned, but I promised both of them I'd be fine. I told Ben how much I loved him, how sorry I was that I couldn't go, and that I wanted him to have a great time. I felt like such a baby for making him worry about me. I watched him drive away, throwing him a kiss and waving to him, and smiling through my tears as his car rounded the corner out of sight. Then I went inside our apartment and cried uncontrollably, finally passing out from exhaustion.

He called later that day to see if I was okay and to tell me where he was staying. "I made good time on the road, and I'm already in a motel room near my land—our land. I'm driving out there after I shower and have dinner. Logan's meeting me there tomorrow morning, but I don't want to wait. I wish you could be here, Honey."

"I wish that too, with all my heart. I can't wait for you to come home. I'm already feeling a little better; I'll be good as new by the time you get back. I love you so much."

I stayed home all weekend, waiting nervously for the phone to ring, and jumping each time it did. The pain in my chest came and went, not constant as before. Each time Ben called, my heart would start beating so fast that I was sure I was going to collapse. I tried to convince myself that I was just excited to hear from him, and because I missed him so much, which I did. But my heart knew there was a deeper cause, the fear that something very wrong and very bad was about to happen. No matter how much I told myself that everything would be fine, I couldn't bring myself to believe it for a minute.

On Monday evening, Ben called from his friends' apartment in Manhattan. Hearing his voice calmed me down, having just recovered from an excruciating anxiety attack. I didn't tell him about that or about my latest nightmare, the worst one yet. I listened as he told me about how happy he was to see his friends, and how they were looking forward to meeting me. He enjoyed walking his land and had invited Logan and his wife to visit us; they might try to join us for Thanksgiving.

He asked how the girls were doing, and I told him about their visit earlier that day. Kate asked me to remind him to bring her a New York sweatshirt.

"Yep, a red one, hooded. Tell her I'll remember, and remind her to keep practicing with that stick. I expect to see her make at least one goal next weekend." He laughed as he finished the sentence, knowing how slim she felt her chances were. "I love you with all my heart, Sweetie. I'll see you tomorrow night. Take your medicine like the doctor said, and I'll be home before you know it. Okay?"

"I love you, too, Ben. More than you can know." I started to hang up, then panicked and nearly yelled, "Wait. Hon...please, ...please drive carefully, and...and call me from the road, will you?"

I could picture him smiling as he said, "Absolutely, Baby. Now try to get a some sleep." He kissed me through the phone.

Tears streamed down my face as I stared at the telephone and touched my lips. Gasping for air, I realized I had stopped breathing when he hung up.

Ben was scheduled to meet with his attorney the following morning, Tuesday, September 11th, at 9:00. The law firm had recently opened their new office on the sixty-seventh floor of the World Trade Center, Tower Two.

~ ~ ~ ~ ~ ~ ~ ~ ~ ~ ~

I heard the phone ringing from somewhere inside my head, having dozed off on the sofa after a long night of fitful sleep. As I picked up the receiver, I could hear Dawn crying.

"Mom, turn on the television. An airplane just flew into the World Trade Center. I'll be right there."

"NO!" I screamed, as I bolted from the sofa and grabbed the remote.

At first I just stared at the screen, not believing it was real. Within moments I kicked into automatic, picking up the phone as I reached for the pad of paper on the coffee table, calling every number Ben left with me. No calls went through except to the real estate office. I left a frantic message on Logan's answering machine, leaving my name and phone number. Then I called Mr. Minton's office. His secretary said she'd have him call me the minute he arrived, both of us crying as we spoke. Mr. Minton was the only link I had to Ben, the only person we had in common, the reason we were together. Together... That's when I broke down, shaking and sobbing out of control. Dawn rushed through the door. I heard her shouting when she found me collapsed on the floor, the phone beeping beneath my body.

"Ben, Ben," is all I could say as I came around.

"I know, Mommy," she whispered, cradling me in her arms as we wept. At some point, she mentioned that she needed to call the school and go get Kate. The words didn't register at first, but I nodded and tried to get up. She helped me to a chair and held my hand as I melted onto the cushion.

She brought me some water and then dialed the number. All lines to the school were busy, so she called Kate's friend Suzanne on her cell phone. Suzanne answered crying. "Yes, Kate's with me. Please come get us." I was in shock and just nodded my head when Dawn asked if I would be okay while she picked up the girls—she would be right back, the school was only three miles away.

I stared helplessly at the television, the scenes playing over and over at an urgent and hysterical pace, nothing making sense, no one having a clue as to what was happening. It had to be a dream, or a movie. This could not be happening, it could not be real. Then it happened again... another plane, and another tower.

Everything went black as I collapsed again. I woke up a short time later, with Dawn holding my head and tapping my cheek. I asked where Ben was. "It's a dream. Dawn, honey, please tell me this is a dream," I cried.

For days my life was little more than a blur. The entire world seemed out of focus, wounded, and sad. I tried to feel for others, but I couldn't feel at all. The love I found with Ben had seemed too good to be true, and now it seemed like a beautiful, desperate memory. Mr. Minton instructed me how and where to submit one of Ben's hairbrushes for DNA testing. None of our inquiries produced any information. I lived with the fear of never seeing Ben again, all the while trying to keep my faith that he would somehow return to me. He had to return to me; I couldn't possibly live without him. Fragments of thoughts came and went, but nothing seemed clear. I had trouble forming sentences.

As much as I wanted to go to New York and try to find my Ben, I stayed at home and waited by the phone for that call to come and tell me he was alive. I pulled myself together somewhat, using a second line to make calls, give details, and search for Ben. Thanks to caller ID and call waiting, I knew where and who any calls came from. My mind couldn't focus and I didn't know what to do, but somehow a deeper conscience took over and kept me going. The fact that I would have been with Ben had I not gotten sick, did not make things easier. Instead, that knowledge brought on stronger feelings of remorse and guilt, mixed with anger, despair, and dread. I was the reason he had gone when he did.

I knew he shouldn't go when I couldn't go with him; he should have known that too. The memory of watching him drive away haunted me and brought tears even after my days became automatic and my being grew numb. Returning to normal seemed impossible. The time that Ben and I spent together was the only period in my life when life felt normal or when normal meant being happy.

This was my new reality, and like everyone else who had been robbed of someone they love, I learned to live a day at a time, each one no more or less happy or sad. All I could feel was numbness and soon that numbness felt familiar and right. The fragile veil of purpose I managed to sustain was overshadowed by the fear that Ben was dead. Phone calls from friends or family were answered with the same tone of despair that clung to every aspect of my being. I felt unable to grieve; I could hardly even breathe.

Dawn and Kate came by every day. Neither of them knew how to help, but my apartment was where they needed to be. Kate couldn't concentrate on her homework, or during field hockey practice. She said it reminded her too much of Ben and she stopped going, promising her coach that she would rejoin the team the following year. Her birthday was only two days after the attacks, and she spent the entire day in tears. We tried to comfort each other, the three of us always speaking quietly, treating each other with the utmost compassion and tenderness. Dawn insisted that I walk every evening, at first with her or Kate, and then by myself while she made dinner each night after work. They both seemed nearly as lost as I felt.

My walks took me past a small Victorian style house where an elderly lady lived. The house was badly in need of paint, but her flower gardens made up for whatever color the house lacked. Her mailbox said E. Bell, the numbers 315 carefully painted beneath the name. She wore a bright red jacket over her gingham blouse, which she tucked inside a long denim skirt. She was nearly always outside when I walked past, sweeping her porch, hanging or removing clothes from her clothesline, or pulling weeds from around her flowers. She always said, "Hello, there," and sometimes remarked on the weather. I usually nodded, tried to smile from somewhere inside my fog, and kept walking.

One evening, close by her house, I sat down on a large rock and began to cry. I missed Ben so much. It felt as if life would never be bearable again. How could he not come home? How could he have left me? Anger burned in my heart, along with the pain of losing him. He let me down like all the rest. Worse. I loved him more than I had ever loved anyone. Hysteria overwhelmed me, and I felt as if I was drowning in its seduction. I wanted to die, and I saw no reason to go on living. Surely my life would end soon; there was no other choice.

Someone stooped down and touched my shoulder. A voice asked if I was all right. I could hardly make out her face through my tears, but I recognized the red jacket. With her help, I somehow got to my feet. I don't remember walking into her house. As I sat at her kitchen table, I watched her lift a large cast iron kettle from her stove and pour steaming water into some teacups. After a few dunks, she removed the tea bag from my cup and placed it in her own. I wondered if it might be her last one, feeling strange that a simple tea bag could bring a moment of clarity. Yet nothing was clear; I couldn't even remember why I was in her kitchen.

After I took a few sips of the weak chamomile tea, it all came back to me. I tried to tell her about Ben, gasping for air between sobs. She had seen the two of us walking together many times and wondered where he had gone. At the sound of the word "gone," my head dropped as though it became unhitched from my neck. It felt like my head might explode as I squeezed my forehead with both hands. I slowly raised my head and placed one hand on the back of my neck to soothe the pain.

Mrs. Bell handed me a tissue, taking my other hand as she spoke. "My dear, I'm so sorry. You must listen to me. We are all in pain right now. The attacks have left everyone shaken; no one feels untouched. But all things happen for a reason, and some day our questions will be answered. The pain you are feeling will make sense one day. Keep his love in your heart. Some day the pain will be gone."

Tears welled in my eyes again. I looked at her as if she were crazy, wanting to run from her table and wake up from this awful dream. At first I couldn't move, and I could barely speak. After a few minutes, I managed to stand up. I mumbled "Thank you" as I left, then walked home in slow motion, eventually reaching my door. The next day I asked Dawn to leave a box of tea in Mrs. Bell's mailbox.

Ten days after the attacks, and during the first sign of life I felt since then, I decided to drive to New York and try to retrace the steps that Ben took on that fateful trip. The night before had been uneventful, another evening of listening to the horrible news and watching the grueling scenes of Ground Zero being cleaned up. The color and shape of a scrap of metal seemed to jump off the screen, making me sit up and stare.

"Could that be from the rover?" I listened intently but couldn't tell if the footage was old or new. Soon it became apparent that things were still being shifted around and placed in different storage areas. I wondered if such pieces of metal were being documented along with any physical human evidence, if it were from the scene. And who knew how far the scene extended. The force of those horrendous explosions and collapsed buildings would have far-reaching effects, most likely even farther than already known.

I would leave the next day. Sitting at home and waiting was no longer tolerable. My calls to Ben's friends had gone unanswered for over a week after the attacks. Laurie and James had been trapped in their apartment without electricity or phone, and had been unprepared for anything other than Ben's visit. He was one of over a dozen close friends who had disappeared that day, with no word since. James said that Ben had gotten out of the apartment later than he planned that morning, and had asked where he could get gas on the way to his appointment. We all held onto a thread of hope that he hadn't been in the towers during the attacks. But since none of us had heard from him or had any evidence that he might be alive, we feared the worst. None of his remains or belongings had been discovered, but there was so much rubble to sift through it could take months, even years.

When I decided to go to New York, I called and told them my plans, and I promised to let them know when and if I made it to Manhattan. Even though it made more sense to go to the city first, my instincts told me to drive to Ben's land and then go from there; it would only take a few hours longer than driving straight to the city. Logan Moore had called a number of times, trying to be hopeful and always telling me to have faith, that miracles do happen. I decided to call Logan and ask him to take me to Ben's land and tell me about their visit. Maybe I'd learn some obscure detail that might help me find Ben, some clue, some tiny bit of optimism. Or maybe I just couldn't face the thought of going directly to New York City.

My jeep was packed with anything that could be used for a rescue. I told myself that Ben could have survived, that he might be waiting for me to find him. Dawn bought me a cell phone, something I had never wanted, but now it would be my lifeline. I'd have my calls forwarded and not have to worry about missing any. She and Kate didn't want me to leave; they were afraid for me, but they didn't try to stop me. We all knew I needed to go.

That evening, as I was scanning my road maps, the phone rang. The caller ID showed a Boston number. The caller introduced himself as Inspector Newton. He asked to whom he was speaking, and then what my relationship was to a Benjamin Carmichael. I answered his questions, my voice shaking, my body trembling, my face wet with tears. He said that a tan Land Rover had been abandoned near one of the docks in Boston. They suspected that terrorists might have used the vehicle to escape from New York. My number was found on a note pad in the glove compartment.

I told the man that I had reported the vehicle missing when I reported Ben's disappearance to the NYPD. Inspector Newton said they hadn't received that information in Boston yet. He told me that no body had been found, but the police had started searching the buildings near the docks, as well as a storage facility on the same block. I could hardly speak as I repeated the vehicle ID number on the title I had found in Ben's files. It was the same.

I was questioned at length to determine if Ben had personal or business ties to Saudi Arabia or Afghanistan, whether he had any personal or business interests or contacts in the Middle East. I assured the officer that Ben had no connections to the Middle East, whatsoever.

"He went to New York to see friends and take care of some personal matters. He planned to return following his appointment that Tuesday, at the trade center." Sobbing, I begged the man to find Ben for me.

Inspector Newton promised that he would contact me with any further developments.

Composing myself as well as I could, I called Dawn and repeated everything the officer told me. We cried together and she offered to take me to Boston.

"We'll have to wait until they find Ben," I said, laughing and sobbing at the same time. "Dawn, he's alive, I just know he's alive. He has to be alive."

Then I called Mr. Minton. An old friend of his worked for the FBI, in their Boston office. He would find out whatever he could and call me back as soon as he knew anything. My next calls were to Logan Moore and then to James and Laurie to tell them that I wouldn't be coming to New York after all. We cried and prayed together, hoping with all our hearts that Ben would be found.

Chapter 12

Nine Months Later

Serenity is neither frivolity, nor complacency; it is the highest knowledge and love, it is the affirmation of all reality being awake at the edge of all deeps and abysses. Serenity is the secret of beauty and the real substance of all art.

—Hermann Hesse

There is music in the air, orchestrated by the wind and performed by the trees, its rhythmic melody as clear as the sounds of the songbirds and the rushing brook. I'm greeted by a thousand shades of green as I step through the door onto our front porch on this splendid June morning, feeling blessed beyond words.

Ben is home. Not yet well, his right leg has been amputated, and he is blind; temporarily, we hope. He can't talk about what happened yet, and he still thrashes about in his sleep from nightmares and pain...but he's home. As I hand him a large mug of freshly brewed coffee, he raises his head and smiles, reaching out for me with his free hand and resting it on my leg as I sit down beside him.

"Thanks, Sunshine," he says as his lips find my cheek, which is pushed out by my smile.

Our mountain chalet sits on a knoll surrounded by trees, shrubs, and grass. Poppies and irises have joined the day lilies, adding bright splashes of color to the canvas of green. Across the dirt road at the end of our driveway, a robust brook filled with large rocks and bordered by trees of every shape and size, cascades gaily down the mountain. Its sound puts us to sleep at night and helps to cleanse our minds when we wake up each morning. Located miles from the nearest town, five bridges and at least as many waterfalls along the way, our home is our oasis. I found the place, a former hunting camp, by accident, or perhaps by divine intervention.

After a neighbor mentioned a house that her friend was selling, I asked Dawn to call the owner and ask if we could see the property. Both of us somehow knew that it was meant to be. We were right; the place was perfect. I was scheduled to leave for Boston the next day, having finally been given notice by the FBI that I could see Ben. Within a month, Dawn closed on the house and arranged to have the furniture from our apartment moved in. We didn't know when Ben would be home, but at least now he would have a proper home to come to.

Buying this place proved to be the best decision we could have made. Whenever I hear Ben whistling as he makes his way down to the brook with his fishing pole, I realize that we are on this mountain for a reason. Life can be good even if some things aren't quite the way we would like them to be. Ben doesn't catch many fish and he throws back what he does catch, with the exception of an occasional foot-long rainbow trout. He loves sitting on his rock, feeling the pull of the water on his fish line, enjoying the nature all around him. He feels safe here, many miles away from any big city, surrounded by trees instead of tall buildings.

When I drove Ben up the mountain for the first time, I described every curve in the road, houses hiding in the trees, and the waterfalls cutting through shallow beds of rock and ice. Both of us cried, overjoyed and overwhelmed, together again. He had driven us up the same road the previous summer on one of our outings, not seeing any properties for sale but wishing we could live in a place like this, someday. We realize that the road trips we took back then, now provide pictorial memories that substitute for Ben not being able to see them anymore. The doctors said it's possible that Ben might eventually regain his sight in one eye, and we both believe that he will. His hazel eyes are slightly glazed over from the medications he has to take, but they still look beautiful to me.

The full story of how Ben was kidnapped and left for dead will be told when he's able to tell it. The FBI stopped questioning him once they realized that he was too traumatized to be of help, and that he just couldn't remember specific details. Inspector Newton still calls now and then, to ask how Ben's doing and with hope, I suppose, of gaining more information. According to Ben, it's still a blur, like a nightmare out of focus, one he would rather not remember.

It's been just over nine months since Ben was found. For the first two months he was in a coma, induced by his doctors to keep him still. For weeks after he came out of the coma, he didn't know where he was, or even who he was. I was there; holding his hand and helping care for him, from the time I reached the hospital in Boston. He didn't know who I was, but he found my voice familiar and soothing as I read him newspapers and books, including my nearly completed manuscript. I talked to him about our past and our future, about the hurricane, and about our new home on the mountain. Eventually he remembered me, and then he remembered us. Once he was out of danger, I arranged to have him transferred to a hospital in Burlington, only forty-five minutes from here. I rarely left his side, bringing him directly home when he was released in March.

Ben never complains or questions me about anything, nor do I complain or question him. He insists on helping with chores and has learned where everything is located, often making simple meals or doing the dishes. Every day he makes me laugh, and he orders me to rest when I sound tired. I read to him often, and he plans to learn Braille if his eyesight fails to return. He's enjoying the books on tape that Roy brought him. I help him do eye exercises daily and he thinks he can sometimes see shadows, never really knowing if they're real or not. He has grown a beard, which makes him look even more handsome and distinguished.

He was given a seeing eye dog named Smokey, who has become more than our loyal sentry; he is truly part of our family. A former police dog, the white German shepherd was injured while rescuing a small child. The child was found alive and well after Smokey managed to crawl through the debris and into the shed where she was trapped, part of a wall collapsing on the dog as he protected the little girl with his body. After several surgeries, Smokey was trained for lighter duty, eventually becoming the perfect companion for Ben as well as a delightful playmate for Kate. She had always wanted a dog.

Ben took to his new leg with relative ease, prosthetics having come a long way with the invention of lightweight composites and computer-controlled knee joints. He often jokes about being the six million dollar man, which seems to put people at ease. We've had many visitors at our little chalet—none of them here out of obligation or pity; just support, friendship, and love. It's obvious that we are happy and that we do not feel sorry for ourselves. Our lives are filled with laughter and affection, nature and balance. He and I picked up where we left off, growing even closer as time goes on. We touch each other's face nearly every time we're within reach, hugging and kissing constantly, as though we have just fallen in love. We laugh and sing together and sometimes dance, or sway back and forth for a few moments, when a favorite song plays on the radio. Our lovemaking holds even more tenderness than before his terrible trip. We are committed to each other, in mind, body, and in spirit, a sense of urgency added to our devotion.

There are times when Ben can't get out of bed, but those days are becoming less and less frequent. When he has a bad day, I bake an apple pie or simmer a pot of stew, filling the house with sumptuous aromas that comfort and sooth our senses. It breaks my heart to see him in pain, and I know he plays it down for my sake. Whenever he apologizes for a lack of energy or listless spirit, I remind him about the hurricane, how he cared for me and saved my life.

The incredulity I experienced, when the call I prayed for finally came, soon turned into acceptance and gratitude. I try not to imagine what he was forced to endure, always reminding myself not to go there. *Stay here...be with Ben,* I tell myself every time my mind wanders to those horrors. I help Ben do the same whenever I notice him starting to look contemplative and distant. The terror does return sometimes; when it does, we cry together and hold each other. It's getting easier to keep our thoughts in the now, a much more joyful place to be. What happened to Ben can't be undone, so we are learning to appreciate that it's in the past.

The FBI report says that Ben stopped at a gas station just minutes before the attacks shattered the city. Three men approached him as he was getting back into his car, planning to proceed to his meeting. A witness told the police that Ben drove away with the men, one holding a gun to his head. Eleven days later, Ben was found in a storage bay in Boston, bound and gagged, left for dead. His leg was so badly infected that it needed to be amputated right away. A bullet lodged in his cranium left him delirious, blind, and without memory. He has since regained most of his long-term memory, but what happened to him between New York and Boston remains a mystery. Some fingerprints and fragments of documents written in Arabic were found in the abandoned vehicle, which was impounded and is still being held as evidence. We have no interest in its return. Ben loves riding up and down the mountain in our new Jeep, with Smokey behind his seat.

It has been quite a journey for the two of us. We both believe that we were brought together for a reason: To experience real love. It certainly wasn't for material to complete my book, although we have joked about that possibility. I still write now and then, although my second book is making slow progress. Ben enjoys my poems, so I spend more time writing poetry than working on my novel. The first poem I recited to him came into my head while we were watching the sunset together in Florida. He asked me to write it down and kept it in his wallet, which disappeared during his kidnapping. He now keeps the simple verse in his heart.

Walking on the beach, listening to the surf, to the birds or music. Before I knew your face, heard your voice, or felt your touch, nothing meant so much.

Two weeks ago we celebrated Ben's fifty-sixth birthday, inviting all of our friends and family to join us for a feast. Logan and Anita, James and Laurie, and Laurie's younger brother arrived from New York. Other friends came from Connecticut, Massachusetts, North Carolina, and Florida. Mr. Minton even flew in as a last minute surprise. Roy and Sally picked him up at the airport. The men made plans to go golfing before he returned to Florida; they both miss playing golf with Ben.

Colleen and Pierce were in Arizona and couldn't get back in time for the party, but they arranged to have fresh scallops and lobsters shipped from the Cape for the occasion. Colleen gave Ben a profound stamp of approval when she and Pierce visited last summer. "Finally," she declared as we watched our guys play tennis. "It's about *damn* time."

Valerie is about to give birth to her second child, so she and Scott sent their love. They promised to visit us soon. My Tennessee friends, Nancy and Gino, sent a homegrown gift to help Ben's nausea, along with a small corncob pipe. Their gift went directly into his med kit.

Claire and Dave brought a special surprise for me. I could not believe my eyes when my younger brother John climbed out of their car. I had only seen my favorite brother twice since he moved to Seattle over twenty years ago.

PJ and Carrie flew in from Denver, which Ben said was his most cherished gift. Their arrival made his party complete, and the three took to each other like long-lost kin. PJ and Dawn built a bonfire, brother and sister both avid pyromaniacs. Kate and her Aunt Carrie toasted marshmallows, offering them to guests as though the little brown puffs were rare delicacies. Then the two of them started dancing to rap music, sending everyone watching into fits of laughter, especially after Smokey joined them, barking and jumping about in his lopsided fashion. Music and laughter filled the night with happiness and our hearts felt like they might burst with joy. The mountain air vibrated with peace and love as neighbors stopped by to wish Ben well and to join the festivities. A friend of Dawn's brought Mrs. Bell up for a short visit; she said she hadn't been away from her house in a good many months and invited us to come and have tea with her soon.

I sat and held hands with the man of the hour, gently wiping tears from his cheeks as he thanked everyone for coming. He was so touched that our friends traveled so far to be here, wishing that our house had more guest rooms so everyone could stay. Accommodations were found nearby, so most of our friends came and went over the next few days.

Dawn fell in love during those days. A single mother since her daughter was less than a year old, she had never lost hope that she would someday meet the right man. When she was introduced to Laurie's brother, Brandon, she said she knew he was the one. Dawn is planning to visit New York soon, and Brandon has already requested a transfer to IBM in Essex.

It warms my heart to see my daughter so happy, and Ben loves that our family has grown to include his best friends. He enjoys talking on the phone with "our kids" as he refers to Dawn, Brandon, PJ and Carrie. He calls Kate his Princess. Soon she'll be having that Sweet Sixteen party she has been planning for so long. Ben wants to buy her a car... Dawn suggested we wait a year or so.

On the night of the party, Ben told me that he thought he could see the flames from the fire. They seemed to flicker in and out, but he could *see*. He asked me not to tell anyone, just in case it was a fluke; said he couldn't see anything other than the flames. He also told me that he's starting to remember bits and pieces of what happened during his kidnapping, like a movie he saw long ago, still unable to accept the horror completely.

After everyone left, we sat out late into the night talking and listening to the brook. At some point he turned to me and said, "Angel... When my sight returns, will you marry me? I want to see you in a pretty dress again; and I want you to be my bride, not just my *buckle*."

I laughed and said, "Oh, my sweet darling; I'll marry you whenever you say, if that's what you want. Either way, you're the only real husband I've ever had."

We thank each other daily for many things, and we thank God that we're together. We don't know the answers to who *He* is, or why anything *is* or *was*, but we know the spirit of love. We have faith in each other and in the universe. Bad things do happen to good people, and once in a great while, there is a happy ending. Each day feels like a blessing, and we enjoy every minute we have together. My Ben has given me the most precious gift I could ever wish for—he managed to stay alive.

On this glorious summer morning, we listen to the warbling of purple finches and the fluted melody of a wood thrush as we sit on the porch and drink our coffee. Smokey is at our feet, gnawing on a piece of wood and wagging his tail. I describe a bird that has landed on the feeder and wait for Ben to name it, a game we often play.

"Hmm, let's see, a speckled tweeter?"

"Benjamin," I laugh. "You know darn well there's no such bird. It's a chipping sparrow, silly man."

"I know," he says, motioning with his head toward the feeder. "I can see the little ridge on its head. But you said the bird has a red crown…it's really more of a chestnut color."

They Tried

They didn't stop the birds from flying
And look around; the flowers still grow
They tried to break down our defenses
Instead they helped our spirits glow

Never more can we allow them
To crumble buildings on our shore
Their evil massacre has steeled us
Against the violence of their war

They couldn't keep our church bells silent
They didn't close our picture shows
Our nursery schools or base ball games
Or keep our flags from waving high and low

We are America—we will endure this
We must stand strong and be free
They cannot take our independence
They will not stop me being me

r. grace. comyns

9/23/01